AF540958

A Piece of my Heart

AJAY VINODH

Invincible Publishers

First published in India in 2018

©2018 Ajay Vinodh, All Rights Reserved

ISBN: 978-93-87328-72-3

No part of this publication may be reproduced or stored in a retrieval system, or transmitted in any form or by any means, electronic, mechanical, photocopying, recording or otherwise, without the prior permission of the publishers.

Invincible Publishers

G-120, Sushant Lok III, Sector 57, Gurgaon-122002

Registered Address: Opposite Kasturba Ashram, Radaur, Haryana - 135133

Printed at Thomson Press (India) LTD

Dedicated to Sai Baba and
my Maa

Acknowledgement

I am really thankful to my Maa who stood by me during all my ups and downs. She supported and motivated me when I was not able to overcome my pain.

I thank my readers who gave me valuable feedback on my writings on Facebook and other social networking sites. They encouraged me to write, which has lead me here to what I am today. My mentor Sai Senthil Karthik's words pushed me to take this step.

My critics, Ramanathan, Mrs. Akila Bharath and my sister Ranjitha, really helped me evolve my writing to be better. They really invested their time in assessing my writing and suggested many improvements in the areas where I lacked. Those suggestions and critical remarks really helped me bring out this book.

I thank all my friends and relatives who motivated me to write. I experienced several scenarios which dragged me down, but with their support I was raised again. I am indebted to my friends and family for also promoting my book.

My sincere thanks to TEAM INVINCIBLE Publishers for making my dream come true. A special thanks to Mr. Ajay Setia, my editor Aditi Saxena, and consultant Ruchika Khanna. Their timely responses and suggestions helped me a lot.

A big thanks to my friend Anjum Awasthi Malik – the author of 'The Twist of Fate',who really helped me and guided me. I am proud to say that she is my inspiration.

Thank you, my dear Facebook friends and Instagram followers for encouraging my writings and promoting them.

Prologue

"A successful married life…? What guarantee could you give for it? What if my life fails again?" I looked into Maa's eyes for an answer.

"I know what will be good for you. As you promised me, listen to my words. Keep your mouth shut as long as everything goes well." These were the words of a typical Indian parent. No wonder all parents are the same when it comes to marriage.

I looked at the sky through the window which had started to turn dusky. I sat on the edge of the bed and took a deep sigh to calm myself down after that hot discussion with my mother.

I had never imagined my life to be like this. Arranged marriage! I used to laugh when someone said that their marriage was arranged by their parents. I sometimes even felt that they were programmed to be like that, people who always listened to their parents' words regarding the college they were to study at, or the groom or bride they were to marry, like functioning on computer commands. I found no dreams in their lives. Perhaps they were programmed in their minds too, of how to dream and what to dream about, who knows? But when I looked at myself in the mirror, I felt ashamed because the life which I had hated was becoming my reality.

I heard someone knocking the door. I shifted my gaze towards it. “May I come in, Mr. Groom?”Swaran laughed and entered the room.

Swaran was my best friend who had seen my life right from college days till the present moment. He was there with me when my life went up or fell down horribly.

“Please don’t call me that. I am not in the mood to laugh at your jokes right now.”

“Why, what happened now? I think everything is going perfectly as planned. Even Maa looks happier than ever before.” As I mentioned, he knew me as well as my family very well.

“Yes, everyone is happy, except me.” I turned to look at the sky again.

“Until you speak out, I can’t help you. Tell me what’s wrong.” He rested against the dressing table in front to me.

“It’s Jenifer...I am not ready yet to step into to another relationship,” I said.

“Oh, please stop this and don’t talk about her. She is not in your life anymore,” he yelled at me.

Meanwhile, tears rushed forth from my eyes. I tried to control myself, but the words ‘not in your life anymore’ broke my strength. Swaran rushed towards me and kept his hand on my shoulder.“You are our inspiration. Where is your optimist personality which has always encouraged us? Be strong. Get ready before someone comes in,” he consoled me.

After an hour, I found myself in front of everyone who had been waiting for me. As per the tradition, I greeted everyone by joining both my palms together and resting them close to my heart while my fingertips pointed towards my face. It might look like a very simple gesture, but it means - *I greet with my heart everyone who is present here on this auspicious day to bless me and my bride.* I then went to sit in the Groom's chair placed on top of a stage covered in red carpet and decorated with fresh flowers and colourful lights.

Within a few minutes, she stepped out of the Bride's room and greeted the crowd the way I had greeted them just a few moments ago. I stood up in courtesy when she walked towards me. Both of us greeted the crowd together once again and sat in our chairs.

Smiles and laughter reflected on all the faces in the hall.

Chapter 1

Ajai Adithiya

Chennai

I was excited to see my offer letter from one of the top banking companies in the world. My prayers had finally been answered. I rushed to Maa, who I knew would be the happiest person to hear that good news. I love Maa very much, more than anyone in my life, not just because she is my mom, but because she suffered a lot for us. Being a single parent, that too a woman, was never easy in this society. My brother and I never went hungry, because she was there for us always like a living goddess.

I could see the happiness in her eyes, but she was never very expressive of her emotions. "Hmm…good!Finally, your salary is growing like you. Don't disclose it to anyone until you actually join the company," she said in a flat tone. Those words were expressive of her experience with the world's cruel face. She had been my inspiration throughout my life and career. My friends used to get surprised by my attitude towards my life, which I had adopted from her. Whenever I felt worried or negative about something, she guided me with her simple and powerful words on how to be bold and positive. I shared my happiness with my best friends from school, college and office. I took a second opinion from them, whenever required.

I look very reserved, but I actually am exactly the opposite of it. People often call me Mr. Chatterbox but still enjoy my company because of my charisma. I am always either surrounded by friends or trouble due to my character.

Writing, watching movies and reading books are my many passions. Actually, I adopted those very passions which could fulfil my dream of becoming a successful movie director, but I never felt motivated enough to leave my career for it. For my family, a good job with a good salary for me was the typical middle class family dream, and I could completely understand it.

I had some commitments that I needed to fulfil before leaving for my dream. An average middle class guy knows that very well.

Middle class guys walk a thin line when trying to balance their dream and career. If they fail, they either cry till their last minute or lose themselves in the dreams.

The awaited day arrived. I had set an alarm to wake me up but before it could ring, I received a call from a cab driver.

"Good morning, sir. I am on my way to pick you up. Can you please guide me to your house?" He sounded very confident. I wondered what it was about, sinceI hadn't book a cab, nor had anyone else at home. It was still too early and I could see everyone fast sleep.

I told him,"I didn't book a cab, I think you've got the wrong number."

"You are Mr. Ajai Adithiya and your reporting time is 8 AM I correct?"

'Wait, how did he know my name and reporting time?' I asked myself. "Yes, but I am sure I didn't book a cab."

"No Sir, I am your company cab driver." He surprised me. I had not expected that the company would send a cab for pick up on my very first day. Officially, I hadn't completed my joining formalities yet, which meant that I was not actually their employee yet. I requested him to wait for sometime and guided him to my house.

"That is my duty, sir. No problem, you come without a rush," he said politely.

Nothing could have given me a more pleasant new beginning than those words. 'Wow, what a wonderful day!' I said to myself. I took my Maa's blessings. When I fell on her feet to receive her blessings, she said,"Sorry, my dear son, I don't have change (money) to give you, and I have seen this acting so many times from you. Anyway, all the best." She sounded so casual. She broke that sentiment scene with her nonchalant humour.

He looked to me just as sweet as he had sounded.Or perhaps, I was simply filled with happiness. "Please wear your seat belt, sir," he cautioned me. The car had a fresh jasmine scent due to the flowers that hehad placed over the rear view mirror. He had a wonderful Illayaraja's song collection playing on the stereo. Nothing could beat his master piece. I hummed along with the lyrics,"*Thendral vanthu thendum pothu enna vannaanom manasula*."

We reached the special economic zone where my new company was located. I stepped out and thanked him. He smiled and left.

I entered my new office and headed towards the reception with a file full of important documents. I was a bit nervous, so I double checked all the necessary documents inside it. They had kept a bouquet on the front desk, which added a special attraction to the amazing infrastructure. It gave me quite a positive vibe too. The lady at the reception took my photo ID proof and a copy of the offer letter. She then asked me to look at a camera placed on her desk. She gestured at me to adjust my face and hair, and I did as she asked.

After a few minutes, she handed me a temporary ID card. I laughed because I was not able to recognise myself in the picture on it. It looked like one of those government IDcards where one is unable to recognise oneself. Moreover, it was a black and white card. Since it was a temporary one, I didn't mind how it looked, but later on I found out that the same photo was printed onto my permanent, colouredID card too.

Many people had come to join the company that day with me. I could see my own reflection on their faces. They were so nervous and conscious about their demeanour. They were all in well ironed shirts and trousers. Not to mention, well polished shoes too. I adopted a technique to keep myself calm. Whenever I feel nervous, I make a lot of mistakes.To overcome that, I tried to concentrate on the things or people around me. That could help me remain normal.

I sailed through the joining formalities very easily, since I had seen all of it in my previous company. I helped a fresher who was in some confusion regarding the process. That was my character and my secret to win friends. I started to love that company from the very first day. Their infrastructure was really amazing. The culture they follow and the opportunities they gave to everyone surprised me. No wonder, the American banking companies were so sought after. The HR explained to us the company policies, the dos & don'ts and so on.

However, when they mentioned that I was supposed to work nightshift,it got me worried. I was required to switch from my routine life style. Initially, I suffered a lot with sleep disorders and health related issues, but adapted to it in some while.

Days passed. I made extra effort to learn the processes. What would stop you if you were at your dream job and dream company? I was placed in the migration processes, where I was required to interact with the clients and make the process smooth for them. The management recognised my hard work and rewarded me with some more responsibility, which boosted my effort all the more.

I started to spend my weekends with my friends, while wewent on trips and lunches. My family felt so proud of me and many of my relatives started to set me as an example to their kids. I knew how painful and irritating it must be to those kids,since I had faced a similar scenario when I was younger. Whenever my scores went low, my Maa would show me her niece's score card and say, "You know how much she scored in the board exams? Now she is doing her higher studies at such a good college. I can't pay the donation money to get you a seat in a college if you score low marks." Later, her fears came true. I disappointed her with my poor result in the board exams, so I was placed in an Arts and Science College near my house. I passed with a good score and also got placed via in-campus interviews.

Every middle class parent thinks if their children fail to get a job through campus interview, it is the end of all opportunities. "I don't know how you are going to survive in this world," they sympathise with their children, as if they have missed the last life guard to save them from drowning. According to me, however, that was not true. Life is full opportunities, all you need is to wait for your turn. I had said the same words to my interviewer when he asked me,"Do you think the people who are waiting outside are losers if they don't get this job?"

Life was going quite well, but it has its own algorithms to keep us really busy and worried. My friends got engaged with some part time degrees and became busy on weekends too. So, I decided to get into an MBA programme. I believed that it would add value to my career and sound a bit more professional too, as when I would introduce myself to someone, I would say,"Hi, I am Ajai Adithiya, completed MBA." Moreover, my family was full of people with double degrees. I had only one degree as yet and it gave my relatives a chance to question me,"Why not do a PG degree? You've got plenty of time in the day." I wondered when a guy on night shift got to sleep? Thus, I felt it to be the right move to keep them silent.

Chapter 2

Haritha

Chennai

Dreams were not meant to be men's property. The dreams of women are bigger and stronger, just as them, and I feel very proud to be a woman.

My world was filled with love and care from my parents and brother, who always supported me in all my decisions. Being an elder child, I got a lot of decision making opportunities. I love my dad. He is my hero. He ran his own construction business in Chennai and had a good reputation in Old Mahabalipuram Road where new ITES companies bloomed every year. I could easily point out his creations over there. It didn't happen in a single day. I saw his hard work and the difficult times that he had gone through right from my childhood.

There, my dream started to take in my dad's business. He laughed when I said, "I want to take care of your business and give you an early retirement." He always thought that I was joking andfelt that it was too early for me to decide on a career. When he advised me to do arts & science, I refused and took civil engineering instead.

On the first day at my college, everyone stared at me because I was the only girl in class. Even my professors recommended changing my major, but I never listened to them. I believe women can be anything in this world. Nothing can stop their dreams or passions.

But the reality was a bit hard for me. I faced many problems during my engineering days. If I failed to do something during the practical classes, no one hesitated to say, "You are not fit for this. Change your major or quit." Someone had even dared to say, "Why are you wasting your time? Study something more appropriate or get married to someone." I always ignored those comments.

One day, an uncle came to our house with a marriage proposal, but my dad clearly refused, saying that I had my own dreams to follow. I felt very happy that he understood me and my dream.

Years passed and my hard work didn't fail me. I passed out of the engineering college with good academic results. When I conveyed this to my dad, he cried out of joy. He immediately offered me a job as an engineer in his company, but I refused, stating the reason, "If I take this offer now, I won't be able to learn of the real pain which you faced. I am going to start looking for a job on my own."

My father exclaimed, "Are you mad? Why should you suffer like that? If you want to explore real pain, why don't work in our sister company as a regular employee. I promise you, I won't let anyone know about your identity." Though it sounded like a plan, I couldn't trust him. "Okay, fine. But I won't join without an interview and it should be a genuine one. I won't join if I find any favours being done for me.If I find something like that happening in future too, I shall quit," I threatened him.

"Look how you've grown to be bargaining with your dad," he laughed.

As per our plan, I faced the interview the following week. It was harder than I had thought, not in terms of the questions, but the number of people who had come for it. I found some of my classmates there too. They were happy to see me there. “Are you serious?” one of my classmates asked me. “Yes, you will see how serious I am when I crack the interview,” I challenged him. The result was not very favourable for me, though. They rejected me in the preliminary round.

I felt very proud that my dad had kept his word. I saw no compromises being done for me. I told my result to my dad and he felt disappointed. He tried to convince me that he could change the result and offer me the job, but I refused again.

When I was waiting for my classmates in the cafeteria, I found that guy whom I had challenged before. He looked very happy and rushed towards me. I felt embarrassed to face him now. “It’s my treat to you. I got the offer letter for an apprenticeship, along with a stipend,” he thrust his offer letter in my face. I felt like slapping him, but I controlled my temper. He soon became aware of my mood and apologised for his behaviour. Later, my other classmates came by and we decided to have lunch together. We went to Thalapakati, a famous briyani restaurant, a few blocks away. We had a wonderful time as that was our first get together since college. During my college days, I had never spoken to them in class, as that was punishable behaviour in my college. I still remember the famous words of my college dean,“Girl-girl talk, Boy-boy talk, if girl-boy talk, then I will come talk.” These words were very threatening among the college students. There were many such rules and regulations binding us, like the students and professors were not allowed to use Facebook or any other social networking sites, separate seating arrangements were made for girls and boys in the classroom, the canteen and the college bus, etc.

Later, we exchanged our numbers and they also added me to a Facebook group for jobs' alerts.

That entire month, I went to many interviews and was disappointed with the results. "I won't give up," I said to myself. Meanwhile, I was helping my dad with the proposals he had received for the new construction sites. I kept myself busy with sketches and drawings for his business. He said one day, "Dear, you've really got the talent. I wonder how they rejected you. Tell me if you want to join my company any time." I replied to him with a smile.

One of my friends suggested that I should try for MBA, rather than waste time at home. I found it to be a really good idea. I could add more value to my career and my dream of taking over my dad's business. I joined part-time MBA classes. It gave me enough time to search for a job and support my dad at the same time.

The MBA class was full of people who were a lot older than I was. Some even seemed to be in the 30 to 35 years' age group. I wondered what had made them study at that age. There, I met Mr. Ajai Adithiya. He was young and very talkative in class, but I hardly got the chance to know him personally. He bunked most of the weekend classes. I felt very amused by the way he talked to the professors and came up with silly excuses for the faults in his home assignments. I hardly saw him alone in the class. He was always surrounded by other guys. They passed comments and did mischief. I started to feel something for him, but I didn't know how to express it. He was a stranger to me. Though I tried to talk to him, he was always either taken away from the class by someone, or was thrown out for creating disturbance.

Chapter 3

Ajai Adithiya

I felt too slothful to pack my luggage, but I had no excuses to avoid the trip to Salem. It was a very important trip for me because my friend was getting married and the tickets were already booked in advance. Moreover, I had no excuses to convince the groom otherwise.

I knew that my ex office-colleagues would eat me alive if I failed to show up. I reached the railway station late. The train had almost started to move away from the platform. My friends were waiting near the entrance of the compartment to guide me in. We settled in our seats and enquired about each other, since we had met after a long time. We had planned many get-togethers since then, but they had all been spoiled by me. It was there that my friend Jamuna introduced her friend Jennifer Thomas to me. She had also joined us on that trip. She looked very normal to me in the first glance. We exchanged a gentle smile with each other. At that moment, I didn't foresee that she was going to change my life drastically.

We reached Salem the next morning.

My friend Ashwin had arranged the boarding and transport to the hotel for us. Jamuna and I had got rooms opposite to each other. I tried hard to sleep but the new environment and the strange happiness bubbling inside me ruined my sleep.

I heard a knocking sound on my door. I opened it to find Jennifer outside."Could you please come to our room for a bit? The TV remote is not working," she requested me. I followed her into their room. Jamuna was laughing,"Hey, Ajay! I told her not to disturb you, but she didn't listen."

"No, no, she is lying. She is the one who asked me to call you." Both the girls pointed at each other and laughed. I knew Jamuna and how she never hesitated to play pranks on people.

I sat on their bed and tried to fix the remote, but I found nothing wrong with it. "We are not able to sleep and we feel very bored," Jennifer said. "Hmm, yeah. I too feel the same. Let us go explore some nearby places," I suggested. Both the girls got excited and we started to look for places nearby. It was still 7 AM in the morning and the wedding reception was to be held in the evening. We had plenty of time to spare before that.

"Can we try Yercaud? It shows a 2 hours' drive from here," Jamuna said excitedly. I fenced their dream by mentioning how tired we would get due to all the travel, and reminded them of our train back on same day, later in the night. After much discussion, we ended up at a movie theatre a few kilometres from the hotel. "I forgot why you prefer movies, Director Sir," she laughed. "Is that true?" Jennifer asked, turning towards me. "Hmm, partially true," I smiled.

"This is my first time coming to a movie like this. I never go to movies with anyone apart from my family members," she said. "Treat Ajay as your family member too," Jamuna smiled mischievously. Jennifer blushed and said,"Okay then, no problem."

Throughout the movie, both the girls disturbed me a lot. Whenever the ghost appearedon screen, they hid their faces behind my arms. Sometime, they shouted aloud, attracting the attention of the rest of the movie goers. After this, we reached back to our hotel and ordered some food for lunch. Still, they were not ready to leave me. "Tell us some script of yours," Jennifer insisted. I was tired, so I excused myself and left for my room.

In the evening, I dressed in a causal jeans and t-shirt, and waited in the corridor. I found that their room was locked from the inside. I called Jamuna's number twice, but no one responded. I thought that they might still be asleep, so I rang their door bell. I heard Jennifer voice from inside,"Wait a minute, we are almost done."

'Ladies, they require so much time to get ready,'I said to myself and greeted my other colleagues who were coming out of their rooms. They seemed to have had a good sleep all day, but mine was ruined by these girls.

I heard the sound of a door latch being opened. I turned around to find Jennifer there, wearing a traditional saree of some modern design. She was being too cautious with her steps. I figured that it was her first time in a saree. She walked towards me without shifting her gaze from her step. She tripped over the hem of her dress just then and realised that she was about to collapse on me. She raised her eyes and looked into mine. My pupils grew wide and I was left with no words. My lips became dry and I fumbled out the words,"I love you."

"What?"

"I...I mean, I love your dress."

"Oh, thank you," she seemed to have believed my hasty correction.

I slapped myself once she moved away and blamed myself for the foolish act.

At the reception, I struggled hard to move my gaze away from her. I tried to convince myself that she was a stranger still, the friend of a friend, and that I should be a gentleman. I repeated these words in my head again and again, but nothing seemed to work.

I decided that it was better for me to move away from her for a bit, so I walked out of the hall. It started to rain when I reached the entrance. Soon, I got some company too.It was Jennifer who had come tostand next to me.

"Do you love…rain?"She had placed that pause at the perfect place,which got me curious for a second. "Who could hate her?" I replied wittily. Again, she gave me the same look which had haunted my soul previously. The same look took my heart away again.

"What are you both doing here? Oh no, it is raining! How will we make it back to the railway station?" Jamuna exclaimed, reminding me of the truth.

"I must stop this feeling growing inside me. This is nothing more than a casual friendship. Once we move back, she won't even remember me. After all, I am just a friend of a friend," I said to myself and moved away.

We rushed to our hotel, packed our luggage and headed towards the railway station. I took the front seat in the auto to avoid her. She placed her hand above my shoulder when the auto ran above some speed bumps. Though it was not intentional, I was not able to bear the pain of losing her. We reached the station.

She broke the silence between us and said,"What is you date of birth?"

"November' 91," I replied with a fake smile.

"Oh, you are younger to me by a few months," she sounded disappointed.

'Wait a second.Why would she worry about my age, and why did this question come all of sudden?' I asked to myself.

"So what...? I believe age shouldn't be a problem when getting married, right?" I tried to pull at her words.

"Still, you are younger than I am," she repeated.

I gathered my confidence when she said that, but we were surrounded by our friends and I didn't want to make anything too complicated. I smiled and took a seat on the platform. She sat next of me and placed her bag in between us.

"Is there anything wrong with being younger than you?" I continued.

"No, I just said it anyway."

"Nowadays, people get married despite the age difference," I tried to convince her.

"But that is different," she tried to avoid my explanations.

"Nothing could stop them if they are strong," I concluded and saw her smile, which she tried to hide from me. Actually, she blushed.

We took the berths opposite each other. We shared some glances but my tiredness and heavy eyelids forced me to sleep. She was my last visual of the day.

The next day, we reached Chennai Central Railway Station.

I started to worry about losing her, but I got a new ray of hope that she would stay connected with me when she took my number. Something stopped me fromtaking the first step to text her. I almost forgot Jamuna in all this. Jamuna asked me about my uncomfortable state.

I said,"I have a headache and I need some coffee."She immediately took us to a coffee shop right there at the railway station. She knew me very well and was always there when I needed her. We had both become close friends when we used to drink coffee together during our breaks.

Meanwhile, Jennifer stole glances at me, but shifted her gaze whenever I noticed it. There was an unexpressed love and pain between us.

Later, I waved goodbye to Jamuna as she took a local train back to her home.

Jennifer and I came out of the station with a few friends and made our way to the bus stop. There were a few conversations between Jennifer and me about the bus routes and the other options for her to reach home safely. I stood with her till she got onto a bus and waited till it disappeared from my sight. I felt very concerned about her safety, since that had been her first trip without her parents.

I called Jamuna up and asked her about her location. "I could sense something between you and Jennifer," she said, having closely observed our behaviour.

"Why would you say that?"

"She started acting differently right from the minute you showed up," she confessed.

'I know why, but I can't tell you,'I said to myself. "I don't know about all that. Call her and check where she is right now. Let me know once she reaches home," I spoke casually to her.

"Why don't you call her? I though you guys exchanged numbers," she interrogated.

"Yeah, but I feel a little uncomfortable."

"Okay, I will text you, but you never shown such care to me!"

I disconnected the call with a silly excuse and boarded a bus back home. I switched on the internet and found a few new messages from an unknown number.

“Hi, this is Jennifer.”

“This is my WhatsApp number.”

“Thank you for your care.”

Chapter 4

Unnamed Relation Ship

Formal messages turned into personal chats. We both started to get to know each other better, and soon started behaving like people who knew each other quite well. Very soon, I found out how bold and brave she is, which drew my attention towards her all the more. My day started and ended with her messages or calls.

We never labelled our relationship,whether friends or lovers, but we stayed well within our limits. She started to inspire me with her words and the care she showed towards me.

"Who is on the phone, what has happened to you? You are always on the phone now," I heard Jamuna voice from behind.

Yes, we kept our conversations a secrete, and it had a genuine reason behind it. We both felt a little guilty and worried about how Jamuna would take it that her friends were in love. None of us had actually confessed our love for each other, but does love really need to be confessed to the one we show it to? We knew it and we were waiting for the perfect moment to express it.

"No, it's nothing. Just talking to an old friend," she convinced Jamuna.

'Friend?'That word went through my heartlike a sword, but soon she healed it with her words,"I am really sorry, I didn't mean it, but Jamuna had started to suspect."

"So, if we are not friends, what are we?"

I had placed a tricky question to her, but she was clever in answering with,"Ask your heart about that or wait till I answer."Red bull is not the only thing that can give you wings, love can too, and I had started to fly in the air.

We both worked in different shift timings and started to face our first bout of loneliness by the month's end. I thought I was the only one suffering so, but soon came to know that she was not able to bear the loneliness either. She changed her own shift to night. When I came to know of that, I felt it was the perfect time to express my love for her, but I was still a little scared.

The following weekend, I skipped my MBA classes and decided to visit Pondicherry with my best friends from school and college.

When I told her,"I am going to Pondicherry," her first question was,"Do you drink?" I had never imagined that she would ever ask this question, having forgotten myself that the place was famous among Chennai guysfor boozing.

"Hmm, yes. I drink, but occasionally," I paused for her response.

"Yeah, that's your personal decision, but you should be in your limit," she advised. I felt heartbroken when she mentioned 'Your personal decision'. I loved the possessive kind of relationships which act as a stethoscope to check your love beat.

"So,you don't care about me?" I asked a bit outraged.

"Who said I don't care about you? I respect your freedom. Promise me, this will be your last boozing trip." She sounded like a wife.

"Sure, but I will have some with my friends at my bachelor's party. Is that okay with you?"

"Okay, fine. I'll allow that. There is one more condition. Whatever you do, don't switch off your mobile. I need to hear you voice."

"I promise you, I won't."

We had planned to take a bus, but some strike was announced in Pondicherry, so we were forced to take a cab. Regardless, it was an amazing trip. We took some pit stops in between and bought matching T-shirts for our entire gang. Everyone started to talk about their lives and recent crushes. I tried to keep my mouth shut, but couldn't for long. They noticed my mobile pinging and the repeated'tok-tok'sound of incoming messages, and I was caught red handed. I had to tell them the truth, which added to their fun. I had always been the one who dragged people into such revelations and then make fun of them, but this time, it was their day.

We checked-in to the hotel and decided to take rest till that evening since no shops were open due to the strike. I told the same to Jennifer and she laughed at our fate. I said, "Okay look, I will switch off my mobile while boozing."

"What? Did you forget the promise?"

"I remember, but I always get into trouble when I booze. Either I call someone up and scold them or indulge them with something very boring. Either will create a problem for me."

"Is it? Interesting, but this time you can make a call to me while boozing, or I will stay on line while you booze," she gave an uncomfortable idea.

'I should blame myself. Why would I confess the secrete to her and get into trouble again,' I said to myself. "No way, this is not going to happen. I really don't want to spoil our relationship," I refused the idea.

"I won't leave you ever, I swear," she assured me. I was still not convinced and we discussed it for a while. Finally, she won.

My friends and I visited a local restaurant called Cafe' Xtasi which was famous for its pizza and brownies. After the evening meal at Cafe' Xtasi, we bought some imported liquor and went back to our hotel. There started the party time with some nice romantic songs. I took a few shots and found myself on a couch. I gave her a missed call to check whether she is available. Immediately, I got a call back from her. I excused myself from the company of my friends and rushed to the next room. We had a conversation about some general topics and then she gave a lecture on the dangers of consuming alcohol. None of her advice went to my head, except the one thing she said about her feelings. "I really care about you and I need you, always."

I felt that it was the perfect time to express my love. I was anyway too nervous to say it while sober. I decided to make that move comfortable for me, so I started with a question,"How can you take care of me always?"

"Why not? I will be with you, right?" she replied.

"Do you think is it possible to take care of someone?"

"I believe so."

"What name would you give that relationship?"

"Definitely not friendship," she said.

"Do you love me?" I broke the suspense.

"I can't answer that to you now. You are drunk and this is not the right time," she rushed to end the call.

"Wait. Reply a yes or no to me before you leave," I insisted.

"I will neverever leave you, but this is not the right time. Good night." She disconnected the call.

I can't express my emotions in word of what I felt when she said, "I will neverever leave you." It echoed in my mind over and over again.

When I went back to the other room, everyone was quite boozed. I found that the party wasn't over yet, so I decided to join them. I found my favourite song in the playlist.'Kathalin deepam ondru', it was the perfect song for the situation.

The next day, someone kicked me off the bed and I realised that it was late. It was 10 AM already. "How could I be so irresponsible!" I blamed myself and rushed to look for my mobile. I froze when I saw 10 missed calls from Jennifer. I rushed out from the room to the balcony and dialled her up.

"Hello, Hi Jennifer!" Before I could finish my words, she started to scold me. I acted innocent and said,"I am really sorry. Did I say something wrong yesterday?"

"Oh great, I suspected so. So you were blabbering due to the alcohol." She sounded very disappointed.

"So I did say something wrong?" I continued.

"Nothing, I will talk to you later." She rushed to disconnect the call again.

"But you said that you will never ever leave me. What happened to your promise?"

"Stupid, are you playing with me?"

"Those were the most memorable words for me, Jennifer. Nothing can erase that precious memory from my mind. I am still waiting for your answer," I assured her.

"Everything seems like a fantasy to me. I couldn't believe my ears. What if I say no?" she tested me.

"I have some more bottles left behind. I will drink till I overcome the rejection," I said to tease her, but she yelled at me. It was the first time.

"Go and drink as much as you can. That won't only kill you, but also me. I love you more than anything and I can't lose you. Please don't talk like that." She began to cry and I felt like my heart had broken into pieces.

I promised her,"I will never drink again, not even at my bachelors' party," but she was not convinced. I still heard her weeping."Please, stop crying for me. I love you, Jennifer, and I can't bear this pain. Please, stop it," I begged.

Later, she wiped her tears and asked,"Will you always be with me?"

"Yes, I will never make you cry again. I love you too."

I packed my luggage and took a bus back to Chennai with my friends.

"*Started, dear.*"

"*I love you, come safely,*" she replied.

Chapter 5

Haritha

I was curious to meet Mr. Ajai Adithiya in class, but was disappointed to see his place empty. I asked myself,"Why am I so curious, and why am I so disappointed now? He is just my classmate." I never got to know why. I gathered some confidence to enquire about him from his friends, but none were aware of his whereabouts. Giving a fake reason, I managed to get his mobile number and saved it as 'My Ajai', but later edited it to 'Mr. Ajai'.I blushed and hugged my mobile.

After the class, my dad offered me a project for structural drawing as a trainee in his sister concern but I refused again."No, dad.We already talked about this. I can't accept an offer like this."

"Look, my dear, this is not a recommendation from me. This is open to all, I just bought the application for you." He handed over an application form to me and continued,"A new guy in our company suggested this idea and we felt that it would be the best way to find really talented people. All you need to do is work as a trainee for a project and if your presentation is good enough, you will get recruited in our company."

"Thanks, dad, for understanding my dream," I hugged and kissed him.

He kissed me back and said,"Anything for you my princess."

I took my mobile out and posted the form in the Facebook group immediately. The guy from my dad's sister concern commented,"*You owe me the credit for giving such a wonderful idea.*"

"😆*Thank you*" I replied back and pretended to be unaware of it.

The next day, I went to my dad's sister concern to submit the filled forms. There, I met the same guy again and smiled at him.

"Look, who's here! Someone is here to fulfil her challenge," he laughed. Whenever I met that guy, he always tested my patience. "Just kidding, welcome to Hari Constructions." He offered me his hand. I shook hands with him and then he snatched my forms."I have a good reputation here. I can refer your name and help you get your profile shortlist." He sounded very patronising, but I refused it.

I then walked into the office room and submitted my forms. They asked me to wait for some time. I waited in a meeting room where I saw some similar faces that I had seen during the interview a few months before. After a few minutes, the HR walked into the room and started to call out the names of the shortlistedcandidates. I came to the edge of my seat out of tension.

"Haritha Arumugam, please come here," she called out.

I felt very happy."Yes, Ma'am," I said and rushed over to her.

"Thank you, everyone, for participating. We've got our candidates here. The remaining people can try for our upcoming projects later. Thank you." She sounded so professional. She then took us to her cabin. I looked around to find that about ten people had been shortlisted for this project.

'The key is here now, you need to give your best,' I motivated myself.

She called every individual to her system one after the other, where she was busy preparing the offer letters and agreements. When my turn came, I took the seat next to her and gave her my documents one by one. She didn't shift her gaze away from the system. She was acting like a robot, without any expressions, but I sensed that something gave her a shock when she went through my documents.

'No!That is my ration card xerox and my dad's photo would be there since he is the family head,' I said to myself and tried to hide my face behind my file.

She turned to me and asked, "Ma'am are you the daughter of our MD?"

She started to raise her voice out of surprise, but I stopped her and requested her,"Please ma'am, don't be loud. I don't want to use the privilege of being the MD's daughter here. Please, do treat me just as one among the candidates."

"You are really great, ma'am.A few months ago you came here for an interview, I remember, and you had done well that day, but the result was negative," she recalled.

"Yeah ma'am, that was a disappointing day," I looked down.

"Come on, ma'am. You are really great. You can take over the entire company at any time, but you are here as a candidate, looking for a job," she said, impressed.

"Thank you, but all the credit goes to my dad for being such an example to me. Please don't disclose my true identity to anyone," I smiled and left the chair for the next candidate who had been waiting behind me.

After the documentation session, she introduced the senior engineer of the company to us and left us with a smile. The senior engineer explained to us the procedure of how the project internship programme works and the date of submission in a strict tone. He reminded me of my college dean. From the very next day, I started to work with Hari Constructions as a trainee.

During break time,the HR ma'am took me to the canteen. "Our company is now full of youngsters. Look at that guy who gave this internship programme idea. He is handsome, but a bit overconfident," she said, pointing at my classmate who was sitting a few tables away from us.

"I agree he is overconfident, but he doesn't look all that handsome to me, ma'am," I gave him a quick look and turned back.

"Ma'am, please call me Shoba," she laughed.

I replied, "Then you need to stop calling me ma'am too."

We both laughed and agreed mutually. When she mentioned this guy being handsome, my thoughts immediately took me to Mr. Ajai Adithiya. I really missed him. I couldn't attend the classes for a month and I kept myself occupied, since every minute I was investing in this project was taking me a step closer towards conquering my dream.

I started to spend all my time and energy on that project. My sleep time shortened and I was hardly able to spend any time with my family. My dad started getting me tea and snacks in my room during my late working hours in the night. Each passing day boosted my dedication towards the project even more. Soon, I started to impress the senior engineer with my work. My dad felt proud when the senior engineer went to discuss my work with him.

The day arrived for which I had been waiting for so long without any proper rest or the time to think about myself. Dad set up a team of engineers to whom we had to give our presentation. That was my first time presenting in front of professionals. Though I had made many presentations in college before, this one made me sick with worry. I found myself in front of them with my drawings. They asked me questions even before I started my presentation, which added more pressure on me, but I managed somehow. I explained each and every detail of the drawings to them, but I couldn't figure anything out from their facial expressions. Everyone looked so serious to me.

"We will let you know the results shortly. Please wait outside." one amongst them said with a flat tone.

I found Shoba in the canteen.She invited me to take the seat next to her.

"Do you need coffee?"

"No, I always prefer tea, and I really need one now." I tried to seek some relief from the serious presentation. I took the first sip of my tea and waited for the warmth to hit my head.

"That's just tea, not weed," she laughed.

"Yeah, I know. But a good cup of tea can fix my mood far better than weed," I said with the graveness of a psychologist and laughed.

"How did your presentation go?"

"Hmm, I did well, but I am not sure what the result with be."

"You could have anything here within a fraction of a second, but you are talking like a regular employee. This attitude is really surprising."

"If anything comes without you having put in the effort, it won't stay for long. I believe in that." I stood up and dropped those cups into the wash area.

"All the very best, Haritha," she smiled and left.

I went back and joined the participants who had been waiting in the meeting room. It again reminded me of my classroom, since I was the only woman in the entire group.

"I think she will get this job."

"How?"

"She is a woman, what else does she need?"

I heard such comments being passed and the accompanied laughter just behind me. I turned to them and said,"Being a woman is not that easy. One needs to face people like you and your friend in this society."

"Sorry, I didn't mean it," his voice and confidence shattered. This society can never change until we change it. Sometimes, you need to push hard enough to assert yourself. Nothing can stop women and their success in this society, except for themselves and their attitude.

A peon walked into the meeting room with a paper in his hand and called out, "Haritha Arumugam? Madam, the Engineer sir wants to talk to you."

I stood up and walked out of the room, while he continued to say something to the remaining candidates. I knocked at his door and went inside. The same engineers' panel was seated there and they asked me to take a seat.

"We were really surprised to see your presentation. You've got talent," the one in the centre said.

"We felt bad for rejecting you the other day, though you had done well. Now, we would like to offer you a job," they said and gave an envelope to me. I was on cloud nine when I heard those words.'We would like to offer you a job' started to bounce in my head over and over again. I thanked them and took the offer letter.

I called my dad's number, but he did not respond, which disappointed me a bit. I looked for Shoba in her cabin, but even she was not there. "What happened to these people all of a sudden now? Where have they all gone?" I asked myself. Then, I saw my dad walking into the office with a big smile on his face. He walked over to me, shook my hand and said,"Congratulations, Miss Haritha. Finally, you have cracked it. No more waiting now. I am going to introduce you to everyone." He sounded very happy.

"No, Dad.Let me work here as a normal employee. Please?" I begged.

"Listen to me, my princess. I've waited so long for your dream, but my decision is final this time," he gave a firm reply. I accepted his wish. He was very happy about my acceptance and immediately called up his personal assistant. He told him to arrange a meeting as soon as possible.

Everyone's eyes were on me. I was standing next to my dad in the meeting room and I could see a lot of puzzled faces in the meeting room. Even my classmate sat there with a confused look.

Dad began his speech,"Thank you, everyone, for being here at this special moment for our company." Meanwhile, Shoba and I exchanged smiles. He continued,"I am very happy to share a special announcement. This is Haritha, my daughter, and she is going to take over Hari Constructions, effectively from today. I request everyone to give your utmost co-operation to her, just as you have give me so far." He finished his speech and started to clap.

There was deep silence in the room for a second, and I could only hear Shoba clapping alone. Soon after everyone came out of the shock of this announcement, they joined her. "I gained a good reputation and business after my daughter's birth, so I named my sister concern Hari, which really are the first few letters of her name," he recounted his memories with tears in his eyes, but wiped them immediately. Everyone came forward to shake hands with me and conveyed their best wishes to me. My classmate came forward and apologised to me for his attitude.

"Friends..?" I asked him and laughed.

My dad then took me to his cabin and asked me to take his seat, but I refused and said,"That'll always be yours. Arrange for a different cabin for me, but it shouldn't be too far away from the other employees. I took this position for you, but I want to work under you till I learn how to handle this office. Remember, once I am done with that, you will take your retirement."

"You are born with those qualities which you think you need to learn, my princess," he laughed.

"I haven't completed my MBA yet."

"Don't be silly. Who needs an MBA now?"

"No, Dad. I need to finish it."

"Okay, you can do anything you want, Madam. You are the head of this company now," he laughed again.

"Dad...please stop." I rested my hand on his shoulder and hugged him.

'How could I stop going to my MBA classes? How could I not see him ever again?'My thoughts took me to Mr. Ajai Adithiya again.

Later that day, I took my mobile out and typed, "*Hi, Mr. Ajai. This is Haritha from your MBA class...*"

But I deleted the whole thing immediately and asked myself, "How could he know me and how would he react to this?"So many thoughts were rushing through my mind. He had come into my life as a classmate, but his attitude had started to really impress me. I still remember his discussion in class, where he argued with the others about women and their importance. It had completely taken my fancy. I felt that it would be such a boon to be with someone like him who respect women and treated them equally.

Chapter 6

Ajai Adithiya

The love between Jennifer and me started to grow with each passing day. Love took us to new dimensions where time flew when she was close to me and it lost its nature when she was away. A month passed, but it had felt like a year. I carried the last sight of her in my heart and it repeatedly flashed in my mind. That loneliness haunted me. I thought that though technology has taken us away from our loved ones, it kept me alive despite my loneliness. We had not got a chance to meet each other since the day I sent her back home in that bus. Her company's work-at-home policy kept her busy even on weekends, which stood like a great wall between us. Meanwhile, I explored more about her and she never failed to surprise me with her attitude. Finally, we decided to meet on a weekday, so she took permission and came to a park near Adyar. It was my favourite place but I never visited it because I had always wished to take a loved one there with me. It was going to be my first visit there too. The place was located under a flyover bridge, and was full of greenery. There was an Ice-Cream parlour there which was always flocked by couples.

I guided her to the park, to what was going to be our first meeting since the wedding reception. I waited eagerly for her. She parked her bike near the gate and came walking towards me.

"Hi," she blushed.

"Hello," I smiled.

She was a short girl with dimples over her chubby cheeks, which made her look very adorable.

"I've read that short girls are cute, and it's true," I complimented her.

Her smile washed away immediately."Do you mean to say that I am short or cute? Why don't you try someone who is taller than I am?" She sounded a bit angry. I understood that my compliments won't fix my mistake of being late and not picking up her calls on time.

"Sorry, I was in the bath."

"I called you long back to inform you that I had crossed the University, but you made me wait for more than 20 minutes still," she self-fuelled her anger.

"Hahaha...sorry again."

"This is the last time. I won't wait for you for this long again." I was shocked by her attitude, but the mistake was indeed mine. I hadn't expected that she would shout at me like that at our very first meeting. I was lost in my thoughts, but she brought me back with her apologies for having been so rude to me.

"Believe me, I never get this angry with anyone, but I don't know why I am now," she apologised.

"It's okay. Let us go inside." I guided her into the park. We sat down on a couple of chairs under a tree from where we could see the entire place.

"I think we need to talk about our life seriously today," she started in a serious tone. I remained silent and she continued,"I don't know how I fell in love with you. We don't share any similarities in taste regarding so many things. Perhaps it is your uniqueness in that regard, that opposites attract, but I am hundred percent sure about my decision now. Even now, I feel so comfortable being with you. I feel secure and that I can rely on you. I need to tell you about my family and their expectations from my groom." She sounded very practical and bold, but I wasn't sure if I was prepared for this.

"Yeah sure, tell me." I had no other words to say.

"I don't want to hurt anyone with our decision. I mean, a strict no to registered marriage," she paused and looked into my eyes.

'Oh, what is happening now?' I asked myself, feeling like I had come to sit for an exam that I had not prepared for. I nodded my head and she continued,"We have two problems. You are younger than I am…"

I interrupted her,"Only by a few months."

"Still. And you belong to a different religion too."

"So?"

"Are you ready to convert for me? If required…"

'This is worse than an exam,' I said to myself again. "Hmm, I'll need to think about that. Why don't we talk about something else?" I tried to divert her attention from that topic, like skipping a 15 marks sum and moving to a 2 marker, but she didn't let me.

"This is the reality and I don't want to waste our time in a dreamland," she made it clear. I became silent and started to think about her statement

'She is correct. I should consider these things in my mind first and foremost. Life is not all fun anymore. I need to prepare myself to face any situation and need to get serious about marriage and love. It involves a lot of people and their belief too. I should really think.' I pulled myself back to the reality and said, "I agree with you. I am willing to talk to your parents and I hope I will be able to convince them too. We can both take this as a formally arranged marriage, where no one's feelings get hurt. As for religion, I think it is just a way to reach God. I believe that all Gods are one, so I have no problems with converting my religion. However, I will need to discuss this with my mother and my family before I promise you anything."

"Now you sound mature and genuine," she smiled.

"Shall we have some milk shake?" she asked with an innocent look.

'You shook my world and now you need a shake?' I said to myself and blew out a sigh to cool my head.

"Yeah, I need something chill to cool down my pulse which has rocketed up to its peak," I said to her in all honesty.

She laughed and said, "I love you so much and I won't leave you. Please understand why I put down these conditions. Look at you, how tense you are. Imagine if you had come to know about these conditions from my parents." She pulled me by my arm and held me close to her heart.

"True, I don't know how I might have reacted to it," I agreed. Marriages are not simple, particularly in south India. Caste, religion, status and such come in between two hearts to separate them from love. Finding love is difficult enough in life, and to make things worse, we have all these systems in place. I could understand why so many people preferred an arranged marriage. I came back from my thoughts when she tapped lightly over my thighs.

"What happened?" she asked.

"Nothing. I was just thinking where we could go for our honeymoon," I lied.

"I need a milk shake now, we can think about the rest later." She pulled me over to the parlour.

After spending some time there, she bid me goodbye and left for her office.

I went back to my workplace too. It tuned into a hard day even at my office for me. I had received an escalation mail regarding the queries that I had missed handling. I gave the necessary explanations and fixed those problems, but I was very tired, both mentally and physically. I simply waited for the clock to hit 3 AM so I could leave.

The weekend finally arrived.

My mobile pinged with a 'tok-tok'sound.

"Can we meet today?"

"Hmm yeah, sure."

"Meet me near St, Thomas mount."

'What is she going to do today?' I was scared. I rushed immediately to avoid her anger, but luckily, she was late herself this time. She took me to the church on St. Thomas mount. She enquired there about the procedure for converting from one religion to Roman Catholic Christianity.

"I haven't discussed this with my mother yet. I will talk to her today, so please wait."

"That's not a problem. We are only going to find out about the procedure. We have got another important thing to do today."

'Did she say important? Oh, no.An even bigger trouble is going to come now,' I told myself. "Important?"

"Yeah, I am in a blood donor group. Someone needs O positive blood at the Apollo hospital. We are going there after this." She sounded so responsible, I felt very proud of her.

The priest was not present there at the church, so they asked us to come back around 4 PM. We then went to the hospital and walked into the blood bank. Without asking anything, the nurse handed over the application form to her. Jennifer started to fill in her details. Meanwhile, the nurse rushed to us and asked,"Who is going to donate blood?" I pointed towards Jennifer.

"Oh, sir. I thought you are. A haemoglobin test is mandatory for all women donors," she said and took Jennifer to the lab. She came out after a whole and said, "She doesn't have the required level of haemoglobin to be able to donate blood."

Jennifer walked out after her and asked me donate blood instead.

"Are you O positive, sir?"

"Yes, but..." I was left with no choice but to agree. Jennifer and the nurse looked at me expectantly. "Okay, I will donate my blood." Personally, I did not mind donating blood, and I had done it many times before, but this had been an unexpected instance. I hadn't had a good sleep the previous night, so I was worried about driving all the way back home after the blood donation.

Jennifer convinced me saying,"I will take care of you and drive you back home, if required." I knew that she had better driving skills than me, but I had never offered my bike to anyone before.

I took a bed in the lab and they injected a needle into my arm. Jennifer came into the lab twice and apologised, but the nurse pulled her out each time. Finally, I went out after donating my blood. A guy rushed towards me and thanked me for having donated blood for his wife. I felt like a hero, but immediately a strong drowsiness overcame my senses. Jennifer held my hand and we both left the hospital.

She picked up my bike from the parking and tried to convince me to give me a ride back home, but I asked her to drive us to the church instead. After some arguments, we found ourselves back at the church. We took an appointment to meet the priest, and I went inside his office.

"Come in, how may I help you?" he asked me.

"I'd like to know the procedure for converting from my religion to Christianity," I enquired.

He gave me doubtful look and asked,"Why do you want to convert?"

I hadn't prepared an answer to this unexpected question, but I immediately said,"I love Jesus and his principles,thus."

"Oh, really?Tell me about it." He wanted to test my belief.

Fortunately, I had studied in a Christian school where I learned all his principles and preachings. I answered all his questions one by one, like in a viva. He then explained to me the legal and religious procedures for converting form one religion to another. I though that the disclosure of our love behind this decision would spoil my chance. It indeed proved to be so when he said,"A majority of people come here to convert for the sake of love for the opposite sex. I don't encourage those kind of people, so I had to ask you these many questions."

I smiled and said,"Is it?" He gave me his blessings before I left.

I came out from his office and walked towards my bike. I gestured at Jennifer to walk away from there. I picked her up from a little way down the street and explained the whole story to her.

"Why do you do all this for me?" she asked me.

"I love you so much," I replied.

She hugged me from behind and gave me a kiss on my shoulder. "Now I feel drowsy," I laughed and she tapped my back.

"That was the medicine, now drive me back home," she ordered.

"Okay, madam," I said and we shared a hearty laugh.

I came back to my house and placed my shirt on the anchor. I was shocked to see a lip mark on it, so I packed it carefully and hid it inside my wardrobe.

Mom came back from office in a while and went to sit on the sofa. I felt that it was the right time to talk to her about my love story. Every weekend, my mom and I had this practice of talking about our office and the other things happening in our lives. I prepared coffee for her and started with a general conversation. "Mom, what do you think about love marriage?" I really wanted to know her opinion on it.

"Well, I think you've found someone. That is great, my dear son. You saved me my energy and time," she said sarcastically.

"No, mom. There is nothing like that," I decided to be sure before confessing anything to her.

"Then who is Jennifer?"She had busted me.

"How do you know about her?" I froze.

"Come on, my dear son. I am your mom."

"But, how do you know her name?"

"You left your mobile at home one day and she called you so many times. Then, when you got back, you acted so wired about it and rushed to the terrace. What other proof do I need?"

"Are you some Sherlock Homes? And that is privacy theft."

"Haha, okay.Tell me about her," she asked curiously.

I narrated the entire story to her, right from the reception to the blood bank. I also mentioned to her the conditions, but I hid the age difference issue. There was a deep silence in the room for a while.

"I think you need to take it slow. Talk to her parents first. Why do you need to convert from our religion? That's not fair and I won't accept it," she said firmly.

"Try to understand me, mom. I love her very much," I argued.

"Listen to me. I have no issues with your love, but I won't accept this condition." She was adamant.

I went to my room and locked the door from inside.

"This drama won't help you. Open the door right now," she shouted from outside.

"I am not going to die," I replied back.

"I know that very well, but I need my charger which is inside the room, so open right away," she said, tapping hard on the door. I laughed and unlocked the door. She came inside, took her charger and said,"Now you can close it."

"Mom, please.Mom?" I begged.

"I told you, this drama won't help you. Leave me alone."

I remind silent for a few days after that. Even she didn't talk to me because of my adamant attitude. Finally, she agreed to my wish. I conveyed the same to Jennifer, not mentioning anything about the cold war between my mom and I.

One day, I received a call from my MBA class,reminding me of the number of classes that I had missed. My mom started to ask me about the classes too. I decided to attend the class regularly and without any excuses from then on.

Chapter 7

Haritha

I felt more curious than any other day. 'I am going to meet Mr. Ajai in class today. I hope he won't disappoint me,'I spoke to myself in front of the mirror, trying to make sure that I would look as beautiful as possible to him. I packed some sweets to start a conversation with him.

"Happy birthday, my princess," said my dad and I heard a pop sound followed by glitters all over the room. My mom feed me some *laddoos* and my brother gifted me a wrist watch. The entire room was filled with joy and happiness.

"Where are you going today? It's your birthday!" my mom said.

"MBA class, mom," I replied.

"My dear, you can go tomorrow. Your mother has prepared such a delicious lunch for us," Dad said and on drawing closer to me, said,"'Delicious lunch' is the only lie I say," and we both laughed.

"You both never appreciate someone's effort," she sounded disappointed.

"No, mom. He was just joking. I will definitely join in for lunch. I've got an assignment that I need to submit today," I gave an excuse and left.

Mr. Ajai had the habit of always coming early to class, even though he didn't stay therefor long. I figured that it was the perfect time to talk to him since it was my birthday, so I could offer him the sweet without making him suspicious, and I won't even feel embarrassed to start a conversation. Everything went as per my plan. No one was there in class and I went to sit a few desks behind him. I was feeling a little shy. 'You are able to make presentations in front of experts, but it's only him in class right now. Why can't you go talk to him?' I asked myself. I gathered the courage and finally walked towards him. "Hi, today is my birthday," I said and offered him the sweets.

He looked at me with a big smile."Oh, that's really good. Happy birthday!" he said and took a sweet.

"Thank you..." I was left with no words after that, but I fought hard to find something to start a conversation with. I failed and became completely blank. 'We seek opportunities to express our feelings to the one we love, but words fail us miserably,' I reflected, lost in my thoughts.

"May I know you name please?" he asked me.

"Haritha," I blushed for the first time in front of someone whom I loved, although he was unfortunately a stranger.

"Oh, nice name. I am Ajay," he introduced himself.

'The most beautiful name in my life which I want to write after my own name,' I said to myself, but gave him the fake expression that I had come to know it for the first time.

"I think you attend this class regularly. Can you help me with the notes?" he continued.

"Yes, I will. Can I have your number?" I took out my mobile with a serious expression of making note of it. He gave his number to me and I started to type it into my mobile. Before

I could finish, his name popped up on my screen. I started to float on air with joy, while he got a call from someone.

"Okay, I'll see you later. My girlfriend is on the line," he said and ran away from the class. I couldn't believe those words coming from my one and only loved one.*My girlfriend?*Tears rolled down from my eyes and my legs started to wobble. I lost control and fell down dejectedly on the desk. The box of sweets which I had been holding, fell and broke into pieces, much like my own self.

My eyes flooded with tears and I felt a pain around my chest, as if someone had pulled out the veins from my heart. I cried till the last drop would flow out of my eyes, when suddenly I heard some voices behind me. I raised my head to find some people standing behind me. I wiped my tears and rushed home. When I reached home, I saw my brother waiting for me. He started to enquire about my eyes which had turned red enough to become noticeable. I gave him a silly excuse that a fly had hit my eye, and went to my room straightaway. It was supposed to be my best day, but it had turned into a day worse than ever. I heard a knocking sound on my door, so I quickly washed my face and went to answerit. It was my dad and he was worried about what my brother had told him about my eyes.

"Should we go see a doctor, dear?" he asked impatiently.

"No, Dad.It was just a fly. Look at me. I look better now, don't I?" I gave him a fake smile.

"I think you need rest. It's too hot out there." He switched on the air cooler and left the room.

My heart was bleeding and nothing could stop it. "She must be so lucky to have Mr. Ajai in her life. God, please take care of him," I prayed and slept.

I woke up after some time and I felt the same pain inside my heart. As soon as I walked out of my room, my mom hurried to me and asked me to dress well before I come out. I was confused for a moment, but later realised that my dad must have invited our entire family to celebrate my birthday with, as he did every year. My cousins and relatives had come to celebrate as if it was a festival, but I was in no mood to celebrate. Regardless, I dressed up and left my pains behind in my room for the sake of everyone's happiness. I gave everyone fake smiles and greeted them.

My cousin Sanjana pulled me by my hands and hugged me tightly. "Happy birthday, Haritha," she said and kissed me on my cheeks. Sanjana was the only person with whom I could share my pain. I always shared all my problems with dad, but how could I share with him this failure? Thus, I took Sanjana to my room and told everything to her. She gave me some advice to take care of myself, but I knew that nothing could heal that wound in me. However, I did feel a little lighter after having shared this with her.

I kept myself busy with my company's projects and helped my dad make decisions regarding the growth of the business. I faced my first company audit and a number of questions that they raised. My dad helped me with some challenges which I faced regarding contract labourers and supervisors during my visit to the construction sites. I decided to quit my MBA class, but my dad advised me, "If you love something, you'll need to show interest in it and accept it with your whole heart. No matter what the end results might be, you need to go for it."

This changed my view towards the love I had for Mr. Ajai too. 'Why should I hate him and go away from him? After all, he is my Ajai, the one whom I love. I could be in his life as a friend, if he would accept me as one." I ended up with this decision. I went to class the following weekend, but Mr. Ajai was not there. I found a memo on the notice board where the management had listed the names of students with poor attendance percentage. I saw my name and Mr. Ajai's name on that list. I laughed and said to myself, 'At least somewhere my name is followed by his.' Without a moment's hesitation, I texted Mr. Ajai, *"Hi, Mr. Ajai, you failed to meet your required attendance percentage."*

I got no response from him, but soon realized that since he hadn't taken my number, he couldn't know that it was me. I wiped my tears which had rushed to fall from my eyes. I wished to see him in the next class.

Chapter 8

Ajai Adithiya

I was the first one in the class again. After a few minutes, a girl walked in. I had never noticed her before. She looked very beautiful and reminded me of Jennifer. I texted Jennifer and waited for her reply. The girl in class walked over to me after a while and said,"Hi. Today is my birthday." I took the sweets which she offered and wished her. Meanwhile, I saw that Jennifer had come online on WhatsApp, so I texted her again.

"May I know you name, please?" I asked the girl and she replied with something, but I had lost my attention to the WhatsApp chat by then, so I gave her a fake compliment for her name and introduced myself.

"Can we meet today?" Jennifer messaged me.

*"Is everything okay? I am in class now,"*I replied.

"Yes, urgent."

'Oh, I am going miss this class again.' I sighed inwardly and found that girl still in front of me. I decided to take her help and said,"I think you attend this class regularly. Can you help me with the notes?" I asked her.

"Yes, I will. Can I have your number?" I gave my number to her. Just then, Jennifer's name flashed on my screen. I took excuse of the girl in class and rushed out before Jennifer could lose her temper.

"Hello?Yes, tell me, what happened to you?" I asked her.

"My father wants to meet you today," she dropped the surprise on me and I felt like I was on my way unprepared to an interview.

"What?Today? But you didn't mention it before!" I asked her.

"Not everything comes to us with due notice. Come to my house as soon as possible," she said and ended the call. I was left with no choice, like every other time she had dragged me into a sticky situation. I gathered my confidence and went to her house. I felt a bit uncomfortable at her place since it was my first time at someone's house asking for their daughter to marry me. I got a formal welcome and they offered me a seat. I saw her family photos on the wall, but the one photo that captured my attention was that of her dad's in his army uniform. I remembered that she had mentioned this before, but I hadn't ever imagined him in that army uniform. My lips went dry and my legs started to shiver.

"Okay, tell us about yourself and your family," he started the conversation. I explained to him all about my family and everyone's occupations.

"Where do you stay? I mean, are you on rent or do you have your own house?" he asked me with a mocking tone.

"I stay in a rental house," I replied in a meek but audible tone. He asked me to repeat myself, however. 'Yes, my house is a rental one, but that is not my fault. My ancestors did not leave any assets for my family, and then my dad left us so early. All I can afford is a rental house,'my thoughts rang loud and I gained confidence from them. "Yeah, it's a rental house, but I believe I can buy one for my own in a few years for sure..."

Before I could complete my sentence, he became angry and yelled at me,"I can't keep my daughter's life on hold till then." I became numb at his words. He continued,"You are not Christian either, right?"

"Yes, but I have started taking the classes,and soon I will get baptised too." I tried to convince him, but nothing seemed to be helping.

"How long has this affair between you and Jennifer been going on?" he asked me furiously.

'Affair…?What kind of a person is he?' I asked myself and lost my temper."Sir, don't call it an affair! Jennifer and I are in love and I wanted to do this formally, so I am here."

"Get out! I won't accept this." He stood up and pointed towards the exit. I looked at Jennifer and found her crying. She looked helpless. I walked out of her house with a heavy heart and feeling insulted.

This society needs a groom who has his own house, a good salary and a well settled background before he touches late twenties. No one cares about your effort. I did some math on my growth over the past four years, right from the day I had started my career to the present date. I had attained a growth of more than three hundred percent, which was really good in terms of my salary and position. Based on that, I figured I could easily buy a house in a few years, but who cared about that. There were so many questions and frustrations in my mind. Marriages in south India are based on so many criteria, like religion, caste and so on, but nothing is said about the character of the people involved, which is always at the bottom of their list.

I received a text from Jennifer, but I was in no mood to look at it, so I ignored it. I went back to my room and took a long nap, hoping that it would heal me after that miserable day, and it did. I woke up to find a few more messages from Jennifer. I then realised my mistake of being rude to Jennifer. What could she have done about her dad's attitude? I decided to reply back.

"*I am sorry, but you must controlled your temper,*" she had messaged me.

"*How could I have pledged my dignity there?*" I replied.

"*If you had controlled your temper, maybe we could have convinced him.*"

"*I don't think so. He had already decided not to accept me.*"

"*I will talk to him. My entire family was disappointed with my decision, so I need to convince them too. Wait till I text you, and don't text me till then.*"She hadn't let go of her conditions on texts either.

"*Okay, take care.*"

The next day, I was not in the mood to attain the classes before my baptism at the church, which I had been taking for some days. I gave an excuse for my absence to the catechist. He was a bit disappointed and said,"This might delay your baptism."

'I may lose the reason behind this effort all together. Everything depends on her dad's decision, but I've got no confidence in it anymore,' I said in my head and apologised to him again.

Chapter 9

Registered Marriage

All conversation ceased between us for a while. It wasn't usual for her to be this way. Everything had changed now, I could feel it, but I was not sure. I had never hesitated to start the conversation after a fight, whether it was my mistake or hers, it never stopped me. But I was not ready to break the ice between us this time. Love makes everyone blind and lets them lose everything for it. No wonder, it had happened to me. I tried to understand her situation, but that silence haunted me. I started to lose my patience.

I felt something was wrong around her. Finally one day, she broke her silence. When my mobile started to ring, I rushed to pick it up.

"I need to tell you something," she rushed on.

"Yeah, definitely!Tell me, is everything okay there?" I pretended to be normal.

"No, everything has gone out of my control now." Before she had even completed her sentence, I felt my heart growing heavy.

"I tried hard to convince my parents, but they are not ready hear me out. I am getting engaged soon," she said and became silent. I felt completely frozen, literally left with no words for a few moments.

"I am really sorry. I didn't want to hurt you, so I kept this concealed from you for so long." Those words shattered all my dreams that I had built with her.

"I will confess, your deep silence and your father's refusal to turn did reveal some hints, but I had never imagined things to get so bad." I fought very hard with myself to hold my anger which she had never seen till then. I disconnected the call at once. Word couldn't fetch me anything, nor would they have conveyed how painful it all was. She tried calling me again and again, but I was not ready to speak with her. A WhatsApp message popped up on my mobile's screen. I tried to ignore it, but my fingers failed me.

The message flashed, "*I am sorry.*" She repeatedly sent "*I am sorry*", but it was too late already and it could never have been enough to fix me. I switched off my mobile and went to sleep. Nothing could have healed that pain for me besides a good long sleep, and I needed it. I fell into a deep slumber with a grey dream. I assumed it was the sign of her absence from my life.

My mother's voice woke me. "What happened to your mobile? I called you so many times," she yelled at me, having walked into the house just the with heavy carry bags full of vegetables in both her hands. She dropped those bags in one corner and started to shake her hands which had gone red due to the load. I prayed for all of it to have been just a nightmare. I looked at my mobile which seemed to be still switched off, but it in fact was not. When I turned it on, a long string of messages flashed on my screen, and they were all from her. They were the same "*I am sorry*" messages followed by some explanation about her condition. I finally lost my temper.

Once Maa moved to the kitchen, I dialled her number. She talked and acted so weirdly, as if nothing had happened. She was even more causal than before, which added fuel to the fire of my annoyance. "Do you think a sorry will heal me?" I shouted.

"Can we please stop these arguments now? I believe we have time to sort these things out." I knew that she was a practical girl, but those words confused me. Did that mean that everything was not over yet? We still had time to fix things? Was she playing with me? These questions popped inside my head. "Are you kidding me?"

"Why would I? My parents are not ready to hear me out, but that won't stop me. Let us get a registered marriage done." I was the one who had suggested this idea before, but she was not ready to disappoint her parents. I was surprised and wondered what had made her pick this idea. Before losing myself in thoughts again, I asked her,"What changed your principles now? You know this is still going to hurt your parents."

"Yes, I know that very well, but I can't lose you for them. One more thing, let us not make this decision right away. I will meet you soon and then we will talk about this in detail."

She had added a lot of questions in my mind, which had started to eat my head. "Do you know what formalities are involved in this type of a marriage?"

"Oh, please let us talk of something else. I don't know much about such formalities. You prepare everything and tell me." She sounded so sure about her decision that I felt a bit relaxed, but then I got a different headache.

"Will you take care of me and never make me regret my decision?" Her voice melted me like a song.

"Yes dear, I promise you." That day had begun painfully, but ended so pleasantly, like sunshine after dark clouds and thunder storms.

The next day, I rushed to my gym to meet my coach with whom I had discussed about register marriage before. He had also faced the same scenario in his life a few months ago and did registered marriage, after his parents disapproved of his proposal. I had been surprised to hear how bravely he had taken that decision and faced those problems. He promised to help me since his friend was a lawyer at the High Court, who helped him go through with it too.

On reaching the gym, I found that he was busy with some other trainees. I started my workout on the treadmill. When he saw me, I waved my hand and invite him over. He smiled and came to stand next to me.

"Look who's here!What happened?Did your parents-in-law agree?" he asked me and my smile washed away from my face immediately.

"I am here to tell you about just that. They are not ready to listen to us. We decided to get married at a registrar's office. Help me with this," I requested him.

"Sorry to hear that. No problem, I will talk to my friend right away. Before that, make sure that she is strong on her decision. If something goes wrong, both of us will be behind bars. Ask her to bring her original age proof, address proof, passport-sized photos, a government photo ID, and you will need the same." When he finished, I realised the seriousness of the situation, particularly when he mentioned the risk of being behind the bars for it.

"Sure, I will get everything you need. What about the money?"

He started to laugh."If you forget to bring even your bride, it won't be a problem, but don't forget the money. Sir, we are not going by law, which would originally take a month and a letter would be sent to you and your girlfriend's address."

Oh my God! Had he started to threaten me, or was this the real procedure?"Please, let us talk positive. I am already quite restless and you are making it worse."

He dialled his friend immediately and had some conversation with him. He finished it with some 'Okays' and 'Hmms'. I was curious to know what else he was left with. "My friend says that it's not a big deal if both of you are firm on your decision. It will hardly take a few hours to complete those formalities. Also, he said that he is available even tomorrow."

'Tomorrow? So quickly?' I said to myself. "Let me talk to her first, then I will let you know as soon as possible. Thank you for your help," I thanked him and left the gym.

I rang her many times, but she didn't pick my call which disappointed me. She wasn't even coming online, which sacred me a bit. Many questions were raising inside my head."Have her parents locked her or taken her mobile from her?" I drew myself out of those thoughts and decided to call my friend Jamuna.

She didn't know about our love, but I felt that it was the perfect time to confess it to her. I looked into my mobile screen to look for Jamuna number, but hesitated to dial it. 'How would she react to this? How would Jennifer react if nothing is indeed wrong as I am suspecting?" My thoughts took over me again. I broke through that hesitation and dialled Jamuna.

"Hello, Ajai?How are you? What a surprise!" Jamuna exclaimed.

"I am good," I said and paused for sometime.

"Yes, tell me, Ajai?What is the matter?" she awakened me from my silence.

"I am really sorry to be telling you this after so long. Actually, Jennifer and I are in love," I said and waited for her reaction.

She became speechless for a few minutes."This is not a prank, right?"

"No, I am very serious and I have called you for a reason." I explained the entire story to her.

She started to laugh and said,"I suspected this from the very first day, but didn't expect such an unfortunate twist. Do you know, her parents have started to look for a groom?"

"Yes, I know so..." I paused for a moment. 'I have already said enough to Jamuna and I must keep my mouth shut about the registered marriage plan now,' I said to myself and continued,"I believe that something has gone wrong at her place. I tried calling her number, but she is not responding to my calls. Could you please check what has happened there?" I requested her.

"Sure, I will check and call you shortly," she said and disconnected the call. Soon, Jennifer called me back and started to yell at me."Why did you tell Jamuna about us? I had never hidden any secret from her besides this one. Now she is really upset with me."

"What could you have expected me to do? Imagine my situation here when your mobile was not reachable for so long."

"So, you will call her and tell her everything, ah?" she went straight to the peak.

"Yes, I told her. What is the problem now?" I lost my temper too.

"I hate this attitude of yours," she said and disconnected the call. I was not ready to call her back. 'What was so wrong in disclosing to Jamuna about us?' I was left without a clue.

Jennifer called me up and apologised for her anger."I wanted to keep it a secret till we got married. I don't want anyone to know anything about us which could create a problem," she explained herself.

"I am sorry. I didn't know that," I conceded.

"That's okay."

"I spoke to a friend about the registered marriage and I was assured that he would prepare everything for us."

"Really? I am so happy. I love you, Ajai." She was surprised and sounded cheerful.

"When can we get married then?" I asked her with a lot of dreams in my heart.

"I am your wife already. These are just the formalities to confess of our love to the society." Her words took me to cloud nine.

"This Friday then…?"

"Only two days left for our marriage. Wow!" Her words were just adding to my ecstasy. I explained to her all the requirements of the documents and the ID proofs which we needed to submit during the process.

"I love you, Ajai. Promise me that you will never disappoint me regarding this decision of mine." She sounded very soft and blissful.

"I love you, Jennifer. I promise you I will take care of you, my dear wife."

I became very busy with the arrangements thereafter and gave the short notice of my marriage to my close friends. I knew I would be able to convince Maa after the marriage, so I applied for leave in my office. I tried hard to sleep the night before Friday, but my absolute delight did not let me. Every passing minute pumped adrenalin through my entire nervous system.

'Your bachelor life is going to end without a party,' my brain complained.

'Don't worry, inform that Army Major. He will surely bring some military rum for you,'my heart teased in response. I slept with the mixed feelings of fear and joy.

The next day, I woke up earlier than usual. I bathed and looked at myself in the mirror. 'Which attire would suit me the best?' I compare all the clothes that I had in my wardrobe. A traditional attire caught my attention, but I didn't want to create a scene in front of Maa. I finally picked a white shirt with blue denim jeans. I doubled checked my documents and cash. I then took my bike and went over to the registrar's office. My friends and I waited for Jennifer for some while at the office, but she wasn't responding to my calls again.

'Not again, not today,' I said to myself. My gym trainer rushed towards me and said,"Do you have her photographs with you? We can start the paper work before she arrives."

"Sorry, I don't have any of her photographs."

"What? Call her and check where she is."

"She is not responding to my calls," I said in a low tone. He gave me a frustrated look and went inside the office. 'Where has she gone? She knows what an important day it is, then why?' I started to lose my temper. Finally, she arrived, but she didn't look either excited or happy.

"What happened to you? Why have you come so late? You know what an important day it is!" I bombarded her with questions, but she pulled me away from my friends and said,"Can we please stop this?" She sounded serious.

I withdrew my arm from her hold and looked her in the eyes."What? You were the one to give this idea and everything is now happening according to your own wish and acceptance. What the hell happened now?" I lost my control.

"No, listen to me. My parents will accept our love soon, believe me." She gave me some more reasons and justifications.

"Then why are we here? Don't you remember that day, how your parents threw me out?"

"Listen, I can't hurt my parents," she said in a firm tone.

I turned and walked away from her.

I told everything to my gym trainer who had helped me so far. I apologised to everyone who had come for me and then walked back to her. "I will get you a cab. Please leave, go back to your parents, and never show your face to me again," I told her.

She tried to explain her situation to me, but I was not ready to hear anything from her. She had already done a lot to me and nothing could make me recover from that. "Please, get inside the cab and go safely," I told her when the cab arrived. I told the cab driver to drop her home.

"Listen to me," she argued.

"I don't want to hear anything now," I said firmly.

I cancelled my leave and went back to office. I switched off my mobile so I could concentrate on my work. I felt that it was the best way to forget my pain. That busy day kept me alive, though I was bleeding inside my heart and that fake laughter curtained my wounds from the eyes of others. A famous quote came to my mind,"*I love to walk in the rain so no one can see my tears.*"Yes, that held true for me and I needed some rain where I could cry out loud. Those dreams had shattered into pieces and her fake promises haunted me. After reaching home, I switched on my mobile. A lot of messages popped on my screen. I ignored all the messages from Jennifer and moved to the other messages, but my heart wasn't ready to listen to my command. She had given elaborate explanations to justify her behaviour and decision.

I went to the MBA class to distract myself from her thoughts which had possessed my heart and my soul,but soon realised that nothing could take me away from her thoughts and the pain she had gifted me. Her constant calls disturbed me and at a point I even shouted at her. It grabbed the attention of the entire class and I was thrown out of the room for my behaviour. I walked out and dialled her up,"What is your problem? Why are you disturbing me?"

"Please listen to me, Ajai."

"Okay, tell me? What is it?" I convinced myself to hear her out.

"I am helpless. My entire family has started to threaten me with emotional blackmail. I can't lose them and I can't lose you either."

"Look, I am ready to wait for you, but I don't believe your parents will ever understand our love."

I lost my anger as soon as I heard her voice. This was the reason I had been avoiding her. "Give me a month's time,please," she begged.

"Okay, fine. I will wait, but what if nothing happens even after a month?"

"I never leave you, I swear," she promised.

I was left with no choice but to believe her.

We met that evening at Eliot's beach. She took away my pain with her smile and a warm hug.

"I will never leave you, Ajai, believe me." Tears rushed from her eyes and she continued,"Do you know how many hours I cried when you switched off your mobile. I was so worried. Please don't do this to me again," she said and kissed me for the every first time.

"Don't you have manners? This is a public place," I teased her.

"Yeah, I know that very well, but no one will notice us in this dark," she laughed.

"Can I get one more?"

"Anything, but after marriage." She covered her face with her palm and blushed.

Chapter 10

Ajai Adithiya

After a few days, things started to change in my world. Jennifer started to act more weird than usual. Our conversations started to shrink and I could feel a wide gap growing between us, but she refused to accept that. Every time I asked her about it, she changed the topic. It triggered my sense of insecurity even more, so I asked her, "Tell me the truth. What is happening over there?"

"Nothing, I am busy with my work at office and I need to work double shift now due to a lack of manpower," she gave her excuse, but I felt that something was wrong. She was always online, but never replied to my messages. When I asked her about that, she started to argue with me. Sometimes, she even blocked me on WhatsApp, but then justified her act with some silly reasons.

I decided to clear my doubt before it went in a wrong direction, so I called up Jamuna to find out the truth. She didn't answer me, but I got a message from her, "*Call you later. I am in a meeting.*"

I became restless and every passing minute added more and more questions to my mind. Finally, Jamuna called me back after a long gap of twenty minutes which had felt like a year.

"Hello, Ajai? Tell me, anything serious?"

"Yes, what is happening over there? Why is Jennifer acting so weird?"

"Weird in what sense?" she tried to defend her friend.

"Why is she doing a double shift at your office? Is there that much work pending?"

"What? She has been on leave since the last weekend.But why do you worry about that?"

"Why shouldn't I? You know everything between us, right?" I raised my voice in frustration.

"I thought you guys broke up," she sounded stunned.

"What the hell? Why should we? Who told you?" I lost my control and yelled at her.

"Jennifer said..." she said and became silent. My world started to shake and I felt my legs wobbled with the fear of losing Jennifer.

"Tell me everything. I have no clue about this," my voice broke.

"Sorry, Ajai. I thought you guys broke up mutually. She got engaged two days ago."

These words took my breath away. For the first time since my dad's funeral, my eyes filled up with tears. I dropped my mobile and sat on the bed next to me. I forgot to blink and tears rolled down my cheeks. My dreams about a life with Jennifer had burnt in front of my eyes and I was helpless like an orphan. My Maa called me from the kitchen for lunch, but I was not able to move even an inch from my place. I felt like a dead man. She rushed to my room after a few minutes when I failed to answer all her summons.

"What happen to you?" She dropped her plate and held my face in her hands.

"She dumped me and got engaged to someone else," I cried aloud.

"Listen to me. Listen to me! Leave her, she doesn't deserve you. Please don't cry," she tried to console me, but started to cry herself. I wiped my tears and hugged her.

"Please don't cry, Maa. Look at me, I won't cry. Please don't cry." I had never seen tears in my Maa's eyes. Even when my dad passed away, she had stood strong like a brave woman, but she cried because of me.

After a few hours, I forced myself to eat lunch, so my Maa won't get disappointed or get too worried about me. She advised me not to worry about Jennifer and cursed her too. I went to bed giving her a fake smile.

I found some messages from Jennifer on my phone. I replied to her,"Your drama has come to an end."

Immediately, she called me.

"What happened? Why are you talking like this?" she acted innocent.

"Don't act so smart. I know you got engaged."

"Who told you?"

"That's not your problem. Is it true or not? Answer me," I shouted, but I secretly wished for her to say no. I wished for all of this to be nothing more than a nightmare.

"I am really sorry. I thought it would hurt you."

"For how long had you planned to hide this from me? Till you got married to that guy without any trouble from me?" I yelled at her. Again, she tried to give an explanation but I ignored it. "Don't disturb me ever again, and your Ajai is dead. Good bye," I said and disconnected the call.

I found some messages from her before deleting her contact from my mobile.

"Sorry, I am damn stupid to have cheated on you till now."

"I don't know why I hid this from you till now. I didn't know what you would feel about me."

*"I am really F*****g girl who let you down. My life is decided by my parents and I am helpless."*

"Take care. I will call you and text you, even if you ignore me. It's a promise."

I laughed to myself when I read the word 'promise' from her. I deleted those conversation and all her photos from my mobile. I walked out of my room and saw Maa with fear in her eyes.

"I am alright. I am leaving for office," I said and took my bike.

"My dear, can't you take a leave today? We could go to some temples maybe." She was trying to divert my mind.

"No, Maa. I have got some important deliverables today," I lied and left.

I was not in the mood to go to office and I had nowhere else to go either. Then I realised that I needed a drink to overcome this pain, so I went to a bar near Adyar flyover. I boozed as much as I could. When I came out, I saw the same park where I had spent my time with Jennifer, and the memory haunted me. I took my bike and parked it at the top of the flyover. I stood near the edge of it and decided to jump from there. My mobile started to ring just then and I saw that it was my Maa.

I could hear her panicked voice as she cried in fear,"Where are you? I felt something wrong. Where are you?"

I realised my mistake of being so selfish."What if my mom had done this when my dad left us? Where would I be standing then?" I asked myself. To her I replied, "I am on the way home, Maa. Don't worry." I climbed down from the edge of the road and drove back home.

I hugged my mom and confessed my stupidity to her. She slapped me."Don't you ever think about this again. Promise me."

"Promise, Maa," I said and slept on her lap.

My life became empty in her absence and I fought hard to overcome her memories. Every passing day started to hurt me more deeply than before. I tried to focus my concentration on something else, so I went to class and felt better. I felt hunger after a long time that day and realised that I had missed taking a proper diet for many days. I rushed home after class that day, but I felt a bit drowsy.

Chapter 11

Haritha

I found Mr. Ajai in class, but he looked very abnormal and broken. He had yelled at someone in the last class and left. I was curious to know what had changed his behaviour and the reason behind the pain which I could see in his eyes, the same kind of pain which Mr. Ajai had gifted me unintentionally.

The next day, I was sitting alone in the canteen at my office, lost in thought. Shoba brought me back from my reverie and asked me about it. I decided to talk about Mr. Ajai to her."I met a guy at my MBA class. He used to be very talkative and enthusiastic, but he has changed now. I wonder what changed him."

"So, there is someone in your heart," she laughed.

"May be, but he has someone in his life, it seems," I said dimly.

"I am sorry to hear that. Perhaps they might have had some fight between them."

"Yeah, may be. But I could feel more pain than that in his eyes."

"If you worry about him so, why don't you ask him directly?" she suggested, but I knew how hard it was.

"I have never properly spoken to him."

"What? I always thought you to be really bold and brave," she said surprised.

'Love can create or destroy confidence,' I said to myself and gave a fake smile to Shoba.

I waited for the weekend to seek the answers to my questions. I also decided to confess my love to him. When the awaited weekend came, I prayed for his presence in class. Nothing changed, while he looked even worse than the previous weekend. He had come to class with a big bread and sleepless eyes. He looked emaciated and starving. I became eager to talk to Mr. Ajai and waited till the class got over. As soon as the bell rang, he packed his bag and walked out. He rushed to his bike and zoomed off somewhere.'Wherever you go today, I will follow you,' I said to myself and followed him. He lost control mid-way and fell from his bike. I was struck with dread and rushed next to him. He was not conscious, so I took him to a nearby hospital with the help of the people around us.

They took him to the emergency ward and the nurse came out after a while with his mobile "Take care of his belongings," she said and handed it over to me. I took his mobile and decided to call someone from his family, but it was locked with a password. Luckily, he had added some emergency numbers on his screen.

"Hello, this is Haritha. Will you be able to come to the hospital near OMR? No, it's nothing serious but please come," I conveyed to his mother. I waited till she arrived at the hospital.

"What happen to him?" she asked some random nurses on the way to the ward.

I stood up and greeted her,"I am the one who called you. Nothing serious happened, he just slipped from his bike and fell down."

"Did he get hurt? Thank you very much for bringing him here," she expressed her gratitude.

"No, he is perfectly good. Even I am waiting to know what happened to him."

"Thank God. May I know who you are?"

"I am Haritha, his classmate."

Meanwhile, the doctor came out and said that Mr. Ajai was dehydrated and was affected by a heat stroke.

"Can we take him back home?" she asked the doctor.

"He is good, but needs some rest. We will discharge him tomorrow morning," he said and left.

"Why is he not taking good care of his health? Is there a problem? He looked very stressed today," I told his mom.

"A stupid girl cheated him. She won't ever live happily," she said and cursed his ex-girlfriend.

"What happened?"

"She got engaged to someone else. Since that day he hasn't been too good." Tears rolled down from her eyes. I consoled her and felt sad about him. Later, she started to talk about her family and Mr. Ajai. I learned all about him, right from his childhood to the present day of his life. I felt very proud of her as she had raised him and his brother well, despite being a single parent. I excused myself and left the hospital with mixed feelings in my heart.

'How bad might it turn if I propose to him in this situation? He has just had a breakup, but that is good for me. God answered my prayers. I think he is my soul mate.' I was lost in my thoughts.

"What happened to you? You look happy today," my dad asked when I entered the house.

"Nothing, I made a new friend at my class today."

"Okay.Listen, your uncle created a Matrimony profile for you. Just login and check." He gave me the login ID and password.

"I am not interested, dad. Leave me alone for sometime," I snapped immediately before it could go beyond my control.

"Just checking the profile won't cost you anything," he smiled.

"Fine," I nodded and went to my room. 'Look how fate plays games in my life. Someone grabbed Mr. Ajai when I thought of proposing to him, and now when he is available again, my family has started to look for someone for me.' I cursed my fate for being so hard on me. I logged in to the Matrimony site and started correcting things about me, especially the factor of working after marriage.'How could I leave my job for anyone? Marriage is a part of life, but that doesn't one should let go of one's dream. I won't leave mine,' I said to myself.

The next day, I went to the hospital, but Mr. Ajai had already been discharged by then. It disappointed me, but then a nurse handed me an envelope from Ajai's mother. I took it from the nurse and opened it eagerly. It was a thank you card with Ajai's mother's mobile number. There raised a cinematic idea in my head. 'Why should I waste my time running after Ajai? If I am able to impress his mom, it would make things easier for me." I don't know when I had become so selfish, but it wasn't hurting anyone and I didn't want to lose him again. I messaged his mother.

"Hello aunty, this is Haritha."

"How is he now? Feeling any better?"

I hadn't expected an immediate reply from her, but my phone pinged almost the very next moment.

"Yes, he is good now."

"Thank you very much and sorry we left early, since he wasn't feeling too comfortable with the hospital atmosphere."

Those replies encouraged me to go even further. She started to message me every day and we grew closer, since I already knew about her. She shared her family matters with me, the way she had done at the hospital. I came to know that Mr. Ajai's occasional drinking habit had turned into an addiction since the break-up. I was worried about his health, so I suggested some ideas to his mom to break that habit, and it worked too. Her emotional blackmail to him added in effect to my idea.

"Today is my birthday. Ajai gifted me a greeting card with a sorry message in it and he also promised me that he won't drink again," she told me one day, sounding very pleased.

"Happy birthday, aunty. I am really happy about that," I conveyed my wishes to her.

"Thank you, ma." She was delighted with my wishes.

The following weekend, I met Mr. Ajai in class, but he didn't recognise me. I had always been there for him, but he never noticed me or my efforts, which really hurt. I decided to remain a stranger and also wished for him to look for me. That hide and seek would add some spice to my love story, I thought. I started to report about him to his mother, when he arrived in the class, what he did there and when he failed to present in the class. I even went above the limit and complained to her about his bunks too.

This new routine made my life colourful and brought more life into it. When Shoba saw that wide curve on my face, she asked,"You seem very happy these days. That's good, but I am very curious about it."

"Yes, I got him finally."

"What? And whom?"

"I mentioned about Mr. Ajai to you earlier. You remember?"

"Yeah, I remember, but you mentioned that he had someone else in his life."

"Yes, but she is no more. They broke-up."

"Oh, now you sound like a movie villain," she said and gave me a snarky smile.

"Stop it. No, I am not. Actually, I haven't proposed to him yet. He doesn't even know me properly."

"Then?" she asked clueless.

"I met his mother, but it's a long story."

"I have plenty of time and no one can question me except you, boss," she laughed and looked at me eagerly.

I narrated the entire story to her.

"No wonder, you are the perfect business woman."

"No, it's not about that. I love him very much and it has grown even more since his breakup. Please, don't make me feel guilty." I wiped a tear from the corner of my eye.

"Sorry, Haritha. I was only joking. I really understand how deeply you love him."

"I can't live without him. He came into my life and dug his roots deep into my heart. I thought I would be able to move on, but that is not possible now." I became emotional. Shoba consoled me and offered me some tea. We discussed many things after that.

Chapter 12

Maa'S Dairy

I felt very happy for my son when he got his dream job. Everything was going well until a girl came into his life. I realised then that he has grown into a man. He started to argue with me and didn't even speak to me for a few days. I've got nothing in my life besides my children. They are my life and my backbone.

Everyone was surprised when they learned how well my children grew up and got good jobs. I used to hear people talk when I stood alone after my husband's demise. They felt I won't be able to stand for too long as a woman, but I proved to the society that they were all wrong. I educated my children well and never failed to teach them what they needed to learn in life. So, I felt that my son's decision would be correct. I agreed to his love, but he was broken and started to lose his confidence. I curse the girl who has brought so much pain to my son. "How do these girls play with someone's life without hesitation?" I ask myself again and again.

One day, I got a call from someone who mentioned that my son was in the hospital. I almost froze to death. I had saved him from his foolish decision, but fate never lets anyone stay happy for long. I rushed to the hospital and started to look for him. There, I found a girl who looked like an angle to me because she had saved him and had gotten him admitted there. Later, I realized that she was indeed an angle, not only in looks, but by her character as well. I saw myself in her. Somewhere I felt that she would be the best person to take care of my son after me, but it was still too early to decide anything. The real faces of people take time to reveal themselves, so I decided to learn more about her. I missed to take her number that evening and realised it only after she had left. The next day, Ajai insisted on leaving the hospital as soon as possible, since he had painful memories attached to it. So, I left a note to that girl and hoped that she would get it. My prayers didn't fail me. She messaged me later that day and I started to message her regularly there on, which brought the two of us close enough for me to really understand her.

She gave me ideas to heal my son's addiction and helped me aid him in his recovery, just like an angel. I was surprised to see the positive change in his life, and I got my son back. One day, he gifted me a greeting card and reminded me of my birthday. I was surprised and was eager to read his letter, along with the greeting card. He apologised to me for his behaviour and promised to listen to me in future. What else could a parent want from his/her children. I shared this happiness with Haritha and she was delighted. That day, I decided that she should be my daughter-in-law, but I need to ask her what she feels about it too. I felt a bit uncomfortable to ask her about it directly, but God was on my side. I found her Matrimony profile online and decided to send her a request through that.

Chapter 13

Ajai Adithiya

I found myself in a hospital bed. All I could remember from before was the bike ride after the class. I found my Maa next to me. "What happen to me? Why am I here?" I asked her, puzzled.

"How many times have I told you to not skip your meals and drink plenty of water? Look at you now," Maa shouted at me, but the nurse immediately came to my rescue.

Hospitals, I hate them. I requested the doctor to discharge me as early as possible. My Maa looked very disappointed and unhappy with me, so I decided to surprise her with some gifts. Luckily, her birthday was just around the corner, so I executed my plan to surprise her. I also felt the need to apologise to her for all my mistakes. I wrote a letter to her after a long time and attached it with the greeting card. She got really surprised with that and I started to overcome my guilt for having hurt her.

My office became my favourite place and I started to love everything around me. I met a director friend at my office and we decided to make a short film together. I kept myself busy with that. I also started taking my MBA classes more seriously and attended every class without fail. Somehow, Maa figured out whenever I missed a class. It was very confusing.

When I bunked my class on some days to discuss the story with my director friend, she came to know about that too. I don't know how she did it. Life started to move smoothly and comfortably for me. The only thing which bothered me was my Maa and her Matrimony sites. She started to look for a bride for me, but I explained to her that I was not ready. I failed to stand firm against her emotional blackmail, and then I understood how Jennifer must have suffered. No wonder, she left me because of that. My director friend suggested that I should accept the Matrimony site proposal, since a wedding won't happen immediately, so I could avoid that blackmail for a while. That idea actually worked.

The work for my first short film started after many hindrances. The shoot on the first day went quite better than I had expected. We did our shoot inside a beach house which looked very beautiful. I took a break to enjoy the view, which brought a lot many good memories to my mind. Then I realised,'I should start writing my own script for a movie. It is the right time. I could take my director friend's help to bring it into a short film. That would act as a good resume for my dream industry.' I felt that it was an awesome idea. I told the same to my director friend, but he simply laughed, which hurt me.

"Don't get disappointed. Even I felt the same at your age but it took me nearly five years to even arrive here, due to the family commitments and soon," he explained.

"But I have enough time now," I argued.

"Let us see. What about your marriage?"

"I can postpone that as much as possible," I said, but he gave me an amused smile of disbelief.

I convinced myself to work seriously on my script, but it was difficult due to my office shift timings and the weekend classes. Whenever I felt lacking in inspiration, I used to travel in a local train. I got inspiration from it and used the emotions and the character detailing from the random people who travelled around me. Everyone carried different genres of stories on their faces and the way the reacted. I realised how my life had kept me away from these things all this while.

A girl in the train caught my attention. I sketched here style and noted the details of her attitude. She was busy chatting with her friends, but looked quite restless deep inside. I noticed a sudden change in her facial expression. It seemed as if she had been waiting for someone, but he had failed to show up and was arguing with her on the phone. She tried to convince him, but failed. "I came with my brother and they are his friends. Believe me," she cried. I could hear her conversation as she was quite loud. As a director, I was required to observe deep emotions before I could create such a character for my script, so I felt no guilt for it, but I always remained within my social limits. She got down at the next station and walked away.

Chapter 14

Haritha

"Am I taking advantage of Mr. Ajai's situation or is it okay?" I felt guilty. I treated Mr. Ajai's mom as my friend and had grown close to her.

One day, she invited me to go shopping with her. I felt that it would be a really nice opportunity for me to express to her my idea about Mr. Ajai, but she took the lead.

"What do you think about Ajai?" she asked me.

"What do you mean?" I pretended to not get her question.

"I like you very much. I believe you will be a good match for my son," she confessed.

I felt very happy about her decision, but my guiltiness ruined it. I was left with no words other than a 'Sorry'. I mentioned it to her that I liked her son very much, but I needed to listen to my dad on this matter. She agreed to approach my dad for this. I felt she was really serious about her decision just like I was. I assured her for arranging a meeting between them and left.

I reached home and found that something was wrong there. My dad looked strangely happy and mom seemed curious too. They were talking very seriously about something. I approached my brother to seek an answer behind the mystery.

"They are busy with a marriage proposal for you," he replied.

'How will I explain my state to them now?'I asked myself.

Waiting was not going to help me so I decided to talk about Mr. Ajai to them. I went to sit next to my dad and said, "Dad, listen to me. I met a guy in my class. I like him very much." But before I could finish my words, my mom became restless.

"How can you do this? I am really disappointed in you," she yelled at me.

"No, Mom. I have not confessed my love to him." I brought her back from the peak of her anger.

"I didn't get you, my dear. What you want us to do?" my dad said and looked into my eyes.

I explained the whole story to them, but skipped his break up part. They agreed to meet with Mr. Ajai's mom. As planned, Mr. Ajai's mom came to our house and discussed everything with my parents. I don't know what they talked about. I was sent to my room soon after a formal introduction between Mr. Ajai's mom and my parents. After sometime, they called me out and asked to offer some tea and snacks. I felt everything went smoothly. As part of the tradition, the groom's family could not accept anything till they came to a positive conclusion.

"We were actually worried when our daughter told us about this," my dad said when I brought tea to them.

"You should feel proud of your daughter. She is a gem, and I felt like grabbing her for my own family," Mr. Ajai's mother smiled and looked at me when I placed the tea tray on the table. She then pulled my hand and made me sit next to her. I felt heavenly comfort and joy inside my heart. I waited for my dad's reply.

"Hahaha...thank you so much," he replied with a positive expression.

"So, when can we start with the next step?" she came to the important question.

"Actually, we got a horoscope match which suits Haritha's well, so we started a talk about her marriage with him, but I think we won't need that now. If you give us your son's horoscope, we can finalise the next step right away," he placed a check point.

"Definitely, I have brought it with me." She offered it to my parents.

"Do you believe in this too?" my mom asked her.

"I believe in it to some extent. The squares in your horoscope tell of your fortune, but ultimately you will need to conquer it," she replied.

"Well said, madam," my dad appreciated her view. He compared my horoscope with Mr. Ajai's for a minute and then asked my mom to bring something from the bookshelf. He looked a bit nervous. He compared Mr. Ajai's horoscope with that paper from the bookshelf and laughed.

"The one which I mentioned earlier was the same horoscope. But here it is mentioned with the name Adithiya. How is that possible?" he asked her.

"I think you got it from the matrimony site, right?" she smiled.

"Exactly!" he was surprised.

They tested my patience to the limit and finally took the decision to take things to the next step. They fixed a day to finalise the engagement and wedding date, after meeting with all our relatives and friends.

I was almost floating in the air with happiness. Finally, I could add his name behind mine. His mother gave me a warm hug and said,"Welcome to our family." I felt like I was already in it.

"Thank you, Amma." I fell on her feet to get her blessings.

"God bless you, my dear." She pulled me up gently and placed her palm over my head.

The next day, I rushed to the office and looked for Shoba to share this good news with her. I found her at the canteen with my classmate. He walked away when he saw me headed towards them.

"Shoba, what is happening here?" I asked her in a sarcastic tone.

She blushed and said,"Nothing, Haritha. We were just talking."

"I know where this will go," I laughed and continued,"I am going to get engaged to Mr. Ajai."

"Wow! Congrats," she shouted out of surprise.

"Everything is happening like an arranged marriage. I haven't proposed it to him yet." I said in a low voice.

"Who cares? Whether arranged or love, you are going to get Mr. Ajai in your life," she tried to comfort me.

'But I care,'I said to myself.

I worried about Mr. Ajai, and whether he would ever accept this proposal.

Chapter 15

Unconditional Love

I realised the pain and suffering that Jennifer must have gone through when I found myself in her situation. My marriage was decided and I was left with no option but to accept it.

"You know her very well. She is your classmate and she even saved your life," Maa tried to convince me.

I tried to recall her face over and over again, but failed. "Seriously, I don't know who she is. Whatever, I can't marry someone for saving my life as you mentioned." I stood firm on my decision, but what can stand against your loved ones' tears? I had to give in to her wish.

"Look, this is the girl I am talking about." Maa thrust her photo in my face.

I remembered the girl's face, but then I couldn't forget Jennifer's face either. What could erase her memories from my head and how could I accept someone else into my life without even loving her? These questions ate me alive.

After a few days, I met Haritha. All our guests and relatives were busy with each other. The two of us were left alone in the corridor at her house. I felt very uncomfortable to start a conversation, though it was I who started first.

"Hello, how are you?" I asked her in a bit of a formal tone.

"Yes, good.And you?" she replied in the same tone.

I could sense her tension and nervousness building inside her, just as myself. I decided to break it. I pointed at a flower pot at her house and asked her about it. That diversion worked well, for she became more composed. I felt it to be the best time for me to talk to her about my situation.

"I think you are aware of my break up…" Before I could finish my sentence, she interrupted me.

"I know very well about your past. Believe me, I am aware of the pain of rejection myself," she comforted me and continued,"You must know one thing before you think of stopping this. I love you very much, but I never expressed it to you. That was my fault. I have known you since the very first day of our class."

I saw tears welling up in her eyes and could feel the pain in her voice when she mentioned about me putting an end to the wedding procedures.

"No, I am not going to stop this, but you should know that I was not prepared to step into a new relationship when this was decided." I put forth my view.

She became silent for a few moments, then said,"I understand that. Why don't you give me a chance? I will leave your life, if you so wish later."

I froze with her reply."Don't be so dramatic," I lost my temper."This is not a movie. It is real life."

"I agree, but how can I prove my love to you?" she begged.

I saw myself in her. I recalled the day I had stood in her position and begged Jennifer for a chance, when she left me for her parents.

Meanwhile, Maa came in. Haritha quickly wiped her tears and regained her composure.

"What is going on here?" Maa asked with a smile on her face.

"Nothing, Amma.We are just talking about our MBA class," Haritha lied.

"Hmm...Ajai, your friends are looking for you. Go and join them." Maa guided me over to the guest room.

'What should I do now? I can't stop this wedding,neither can I wholeheartedly start my life with Haritha.' I got lost in my own thoughts.

"She looks so gorgeous, Ajai.You are so lucky," Swaran said to me.

"Thank you," I gave him a fake response because my mind was occupied with something else entirely.

Chapter 16

Haritha

A mysterious happiness filled my heart, along with the fear of rejection that I might face from Mr. Ajai.

"What if he rejects this marriage? How will I face him?" Such questions haunted me. The awaited moment finally arrived. I met Mr. Ajai at my house. Both of us were left alone in the corridor. I felt both romance and fear in my heart. He started the conversation formally, and I replied to him in the same way. I felt very nervous while he was with me.

Continuing our conversation further, he mentioned his break up to me. I felt that it was the right time to express my love to him, so I interrupted him. I struggled hard to express my love to him. I even agreed to leave him after our marriage if he wished so, but he misunderstood it.

He took it as me being dramatic. I was left with no words, and tears rushed forth from my eyes. I shifted my gaze when I heard the voice of Mr. Ajai's mother, and wiped my tears before she could see them. She sent Ajai away to meet his friends and came to sit next to me.

"I know you are crying." She had spotted my tears.

"No, Amma. There is nothing like that," I tried to hide it still.

“I have been through your age, Haritha, and I know my son well too,” she consoled me.

“He is not ready yet to move on from his past,” I said, trying to reign in my weeping.

“He lost everything in his life. Everyone he loved left him to be lonely. That is why, sometimes he tries to stay away, even from me. I can assure you that he has no feelings for Jennifer in his heart anymore, but the fear of losing is still there. I believe only you can make him recover from this. You are the best that I can give my son,” she explained and comforted me.

Her words helped me overcome my pain. The engagement and the wedding dates was fixed by the two families gathered at my house. ‘15th June is going to be a memorable day in my life,’I said to myself. I believed that my love for Mr. Ajai would bring him to me someday. I prayed for that day to come soon.

Mr. Ajai’s mother and my parents took me along to the printer’s shop to select the invitation cards for the wedding. I asked his mother about him. She told me that he had left home early that morning for a shooting. I became curious to know more about that.

“Mr. Ajai is a director?” I asked her.

“Oh, stop calling him Mr. Ajai. He is your fiancé and would be your husband soon. Yes, he calls himself a director,” she said.

“Sure, I won’t call him that anymore,” I said and blushed.

I got some YouTube links from her to watch what he had worked on before. I was impressed by his talent.‘I believe he will become a famous director one day, and I will help him achieve his goal,’I said to myself. My mom drew me back from my thoughts. They placed quite a few options of invitation cards in front of me to choose and finalise. A white card with the figure of a couple on it captured my attention. I picked the card and looked at it closely. Two figures, a bride and a groom, had half a heart each in their hands, waiting to offer it to the other. It looked so perfect for my own love story. When I opened the card, both of those pieces of the heart came together to join and make the heart whole. I felt it to be the perfect card for my wedding. When I finalised it, Ajai's mom gave me a smile as if she had read my mind, and I blushed again.

The next day, I went of office to complete all the pending work before taking leave for my wedding. Shoba came to my cabin with sweets."I've got good news for you," she said, blushing more than I was.

"What is it?" I asked her.

"I confessed about my love to my parents and they agreed," she surprised me.

"What? Who is the lucky one?" I asked curiously.

"Your classmate," she blushed again.

"I knew this would happen, but this is so fast. I should take classes from you on this, Miss Love Guru," I laughed.

"I need a day's leave tomorrow to spend with him. Please, help me," she requested.

"Oh, where is he? Call him inside. It is very bad that he is using you to get leave from me," I disapproved mockingly.

"Haritha, he didn't ask me to do this. I wish to take him to a movie tomorrow. Sorry." She believed that I was actually angry.

"Hahaha...I am just playing with you. You are my best friend, Shoba. It is no problem, you guys can take a leave. I will manage," I assured her and saw her heave a sigh of relief.

"You really scared me," she patted my shoulder playfully.

'I wish I could get a chance to watch a movie with Ajai, or get some time to spend with him at least. It is too much to expect. I haven't even gotten him interested in me yet," I pitied myself.

Chapter 17

the Dream Wedding

I stepped out of the car and found my name along with Ajai's on the welcome board. Ajai's mom came and welcomed me into the wedding hall. I felt shy to face the huge crowd that had gathered there for us. I searched for Ajai, but he disappointed me with his absence.

"Ajai is in his room. Wait for a few minutes, he will be here," Ajai's mom said and laughed.

I blushed and went inside the room assigned to me to prepare for the pre-wedding reception.

"Congrats, dear," Sanjana hugged me.

"Thank you. Please stay with me till the wedding," I requested her.

"Hmm…yeah, you won't need me after the wedding," she teased me and laughed out.

"How long are you going to make my son wait? Come soon, Haritha. Everyone is waiting for you," Ajai's mom reminded me.

I walked out of the room, brimming with shy smiles, and headed towards the stage. Ajai stood up. Tears rushed to my eyes as I saw my love story turning into reality. 'Thank you,God,'I whispered under my breath,'for making my dream come true.' We both took our seats on the stage. Everyone got busy with the engagement rituals, but my thoughts were filled only with Ajai and my dreams about living a life with my love. Only one night remained before I was to become his wife officially, but I had already started to live with him in my heart.

The priest asked us to exchange the garlands and the rings. He took my hand in his to put the ring on. Instantaneously, everything else besides him faded away from my sight. 'I will never disappoint you and I will love you till my last breath, Ajai. I promise you that, I swear by my soul,' I said to myself.

Then, Ajai's mom handed me a saree that I would have to wear at the reception, while my dad gave Ajai a suit. It pained me to move away from him, but I was eager to see him in that light grey suit and the baby pink shirt that we had presented him with. I had already imagined him in it numerous times. I dressed myself in the candy-coloured silk saree that Ajai's mom and I had selected for me for the reception.

When I saw Ajai return, wearing that light grey suit, I froze. He looked more handsome than I had imagined. We exchanged the garlands again and took our seats. Everyone came to us one after the other to convey their good wishes for our future. I introduced my friends and family to him. He greeted them all with a warm smile.

"You are a really lucky girl," my friends complimented me.

Ajai never hesitated from touching the feet of the elders in my family and seek their blessings, while they were very pleased to see his humble nature. I saw a smile on his face after a long time. I don't know what had brought it exactly. He had not been ready to smile for the photographs only a few minutes before when we had exchanged the rings, but everything changed soon. He invited me to dance with him. I gave my hand in his and danced with him. I pinched myself to assure myself that it was not a dream. I became eager to know what had brought about this change in him.

Both of us got exhausted after the endless photographs with and greetings from everyone who had come to attend the ceremony. We had our first dinner together. His friends forced him to feed me sweets and eagerly clicked snaps when he did. He teased me when I tried to feed him back.

I went back to my room with these pleasant memories in my heart.

"Girls, sleep soon. We need to get up early tomorrow morning to prepare for the wedding," my mom advised me and my friends.

"Okay, aunty," Shoba replied.

"Yes, Haritha, you need to sleep well today. You've got a lot of work to do tomorrow," Sanjana laughed.

"Oh please shut up, Sanjana," I blushed.

Sleep evaded me because the thrill and happiness for the next day bubbled inside my heart, but the rest of my friends soon fell into deep sleep. I lightly kicked at Sanjana who had promised to give me some ideas regarding the wedding night. I heard a knocking sound at the door. I checked the clock for time. It was midnight, leaving us three full hours before the pre-wedding rituals were to start early in the morning. I wondered who could it be at the door at that time in the night. I undid the door latch and was surprised to see Ajai outside.

"Sorry to disturb you. Can we talk for some time?" he asked me.

"Yeah, sure. Give me a minute," I said and quietly went inside to check my appearance in the mirror.

He guided me up to the terrace. I found it difficult to walk up the staircase in the dark, but he held my hand all through and guided me. Cool breeze hit my face as I found myself on the terrace from where I was able to see the beautiful night landscape of the city. Ajai's presence had made that place feel quite romantic, for I might have ended up screaming out of fear had I been alone.

"I needed to talk to you, so I brought you here," he started the conversation.

"Yes, tell me?" I nodded.

"My mom yelled at me for being so grumpy during the photo shoot. I then realised how much I might have hurt you. I am sorry for being like that," he apologised.

"I can understand your situation very well, and thank you for treating my friends and family well," I expressed my gratitude.

"Thank you for understanding me. Could you please give me some time to recover from my past? Meanwhile, we can build our relationship by trying to understand each other," he suggested.

I have no words to explain how pleasant he sounded. He pulled me out from my guilt with those words. "Anything for you," I confessed.

"Let's just be good friends till I am ready to step into married life?" He forwarded his hand to me.

I was left with no choice but to agree with his terms, though I hated the word 'friends'. We both walked down to room through the same dark staircase. I stepped on a slipper spot in the stair and he grabbed my waist when I was about to fall.

"Be careful, Haritha," he advised.

I smiled and walked into my room before someone could spot us. I latched the door shut and went to sit next to Sanjana.

"You asked me for ideas for your first night, but I think you already know more than I do," she laughed.

"Shush... be quite, Sanjana. What if Shoba finds out?" I warned her.

"I won't take it the wrong way if you teach me as well," Shoba said, rising up from her bed.

"You girls are too bad," I laughed and covered my face in embarrassment.

We slept after sharing some gossip and stories about the wedding night. Again, I heard a knocking sound on the door. My eyelids still felt too heavy from the sleep.

"Haritha? Girls? Open the door. It's late," my mom yelled.

I realised it was 4 a.m. in the morning. I rushed to the door and unlocked it.

"Look how careless you are! I told you that the girls and you need to wake up early, right?" she yelled at me.

"Sorry, mom. We will be ready soon," I apologised. The girls were still in bed.

Mom rushed into the room shouting Sanjana and Shoba's names loudly, and murmuring,"Even the groom woke up early. I don't know what she is going to do at her mother-in-law's house. All this is because of her dad."

'Ajai woke up early?'I asked myself with surprise. How could I have told her that it was he who didn't let me sleep in the first place?

After an hour, I found myself in front of the elder women

of my family. They applied sandalwood paste and turmeric on my forehead, cheeks and hands as part of a ritual. Then, I walked to a stage and greeted everyone. Elders from Ajai's family handed me the wedding saree, while Ajai got the traditional dhoti and shirt from my parents.

"Don't waste time. Come back quickly. The auspicious time window is about to end," the priest cautioned us.

They always say the same thing at every wedding. I wondered whose fault it was then. I dressed up in that wedding saree as quickly as I could and went to the wedding stage. I found Ajai already there in front of the '*yagya kundam*' – the holy fire around which the wedding rituals are completed. I couldn't understand how he always managed to get ready sooner than me. With each step that I took, I realised my dreams coming true. I took my seat to the left of Ajai, as guide by the priest. The brides are always seated to the left, symbolic of sharing the groom's heart.

I joined my palms together over my heart, while Ajai tied the *Mangalyam* (a thin yellow thread coated in turmeric and considered to be the wedding chain in south India) around my neck. Finally, we had become husband and wife. Flowers and turmeric coated rice were showered over us. We thanked everyone for their blessings.

Ajai's mom kissed me on my forehead and said,"Welcome, my dear."

We fell on our parents' feet to seek blessings from them. My dad raised Ajai up and hugged him.

"Please take care of my princess," he said to Ajai.

"I promise you that," he replied him.

Then, my dad hugged me. Till that moment, I had not realised that I would have to leave my family behind after this wedding. Tears rolled down from my eyes. Immediately, my dad started to cry too. Every woman comes across this painful moment in her life. Though I knew Ajai's family very well by then, I felt an inexplicable sadness for leaving my own family behind.

"Please don't cry, she is not going anywhere away from us. She will be able to come home whenever we wish to see her," my mom consoled my dad.

"Yes, dad. Please don't cry," I played my part to console him too, though I was not able to control my own emotions.

"We will be staying at your place for a few days after the wedding, and will come back whenever you want us to," Ajai promised my dad.

My dad wiped his tears and smiled at us. I felt really lucky to have Ajai in my life, and to see what a good human being he really was.

Chapter 17

Ajai Adithiya

My engagement ceremony began with some rituals. Everyone looked very happy and busy with the event. I had never seen my Maa so happy before. I realised that I needed to get over my past, at least for the loved ones around me and for Haritha. I exchanged the garland and the engagement ring with her.

'You should never let your past ruin your present,' I said to myself.

I walked into my room to get dressed for the wedding reception. I placed the shirt and suit on the bed.

"Only my Maa can select such colours for me," I complained to Swaran.

"Why? What is wrong with the colour? It really suits you," Swaran argued.

Meanwhile, Maa entered the room, looking furious. I knew she was not happy with my behaviour during the rituals.

"What do you think of yourself? Do you even know how much she loves you?" she yelled at me.

"Maa, listen to me," I tried to interrupt her, but failed.

"Had it been any other girl in her position, she would have cancelled this wedding. Who will accept you after getting to know about your break up? Haritha is a gem and we should feel lucky to have her. I see no difference between you and your stupid ex-girlfriend, who left you without realising true love," she sounded more furious than I had thought.

'Yes, she is correct. I must respect Haritha's love, but I need time,'I said to myself and decided to talk to Haritha after the engagement ceremony.

"Sorry, Maa. I was just a bit nervous. There is nothing besides that," I tried to convince her.

"Whatever, at least try to smile to make her feel comfortable," she suggested and walked out of the room.

"Don't take me mistakenly, you are always the one to guide us, but I think you need to listen to me this time. Your mom is right and I think Haritha is a really good person. Try to get over your past and help yourself the same way you helped me," Swaran advised, reminding me of my own words that I had said to him when he underwent this break up.

"I agree with you and I have already decided to forget my past. Thank you, Swaran," I said.

I walked out of the room, fully dressed, and waited for Haritha at the stage. She soon arrived, looking gorgeous in a traditional silk saree. Had I met her before Jennifer, the story might have been so different. She looked like an angel and when she blushed, it added even more beauty to her being. She reminded me of some words I had read somewhere before,'She doesn't need lip gloss to impress me, a warm smile can make it happen.'

I had decided to talk to Haritha after the engagement, but friends and family kept me completely occupied. Finally, everyone went to sleep and I gained the confidence to walk over to her room. I knocked at the door and prayer for her to open it. I felt lucky when she did, as I was not prepared to answer to anyone else.

I took her up to the terrace and apologised for my attitude. I felt relieved when she gracefully accepted it. I also requested her for some time to recover from my past, and we agreed to be friends till then. I realized she got uncomfortable when I mentioned the word 'friends', but I had no other option to offer.

She had a minor slip while climbing down to her room. I rushed to hold her. While at it, I noticed her beautiful dark eyes and lost myself in her fragrance. It awakened my manhood inside me.

Wewalked back to our respective rooms quietly. The next day, I found myself in front of the ceremonial wedding fire. The priest recited some prayers and asked me to repeat some chants after him. I found it quite difficult to pronounce all those Sanskrit words.

Everyone showered us with flowers and *archathai* (turmeric-coated rice) to bless us. We had become man and wife.

I felt both nervous and curious about living a married life.

Haritha guided me to her room the next day and offered me to take rest. I felt quite uncomfortable staying at her house, but I had promised her dad that we would. A womanly fragrance filled her room, which was new to me since I had never experienced it back home. A typical bachelor's room, as the one that I had, smelled mostly of sweat and unwashed towels.

"May I come in?" Haritha knocked at the door.

"Yes," I laughed.

"Why are you laughing?" she asked me.

"This is your room. I am a guest here."

"No, you are my husband and you have all the right to stay here," she reminded me.

I smiled as she offered me a cup of tea.

"I prefer coffee actually, strong with half sugar," I told her.

"Oh, I am sorry. I will bring coffee for you," she said and left.

Meanwhile, my attention was caught by the beautiful paintings and photo frames on the walls of her room.

"Those are my childhood photographs," she said when she came back with a fresh cup of coffee for me.

"Really? You look adorable."

"Thank you," she blushed.

I took the coffee from her and walked over to the door. She rushed to stand in my path. I sensed that she was trying to hide something from me. Out of a growing curiosity, I place the cup on the table next to me and tried to move her aside. She turned towards the door and tore something that had been pasted on it. I pulled her around, but she lost her balance and fell on me. Our eyes met and I felt her heartbeat rising. The same fragrance which had aroused my manhood before, did its magic again. I couldn't control my emotions, while her beautiful eyes fuelled it even more.

'What is this? How could I be so perverted?'I asked myself and felt that it was not right to take advantage of her, so I simply helped her get up. An awkward silence grew between us. She walked out of the room, but dropped the paper which she had torn from the door. I picked it up as soon as she was out of sight. It was a picture of me. She had drawn hearts over it and had also written'I love you' on it.

I gulped down the last few sips of coffee left in the cup and kept it aside. Then, I pasted that picture back at its place.

Chapter 18

Behind the Imaginary walls

I was really happy to see Ajai at my home. I believed that one day he would understand my love and the wall between us would fall. I introduced my neighbours, who came to meet us, to Ajai. I then took Ajai back to my room.

"Feel free and take rest. I will be back soon," I said to Ajai and went to the kitchen. There, I prepared tea for him and came back to my room with it. However, when I came to know that he preferred coffee, I went back to the kitchen to bring it for him. When I entered back into the room the second time, I saw Ajai busy enjoying the paintings and photos on the wall. I pointed out my childhood photos to him and offered him the fresh cup of coffee.

I caught sight of Ajai's photo suddenly which I had pasted behind the door to see him daily, but prevent others from noticing it. I rushed to the door to tear it off before Ajai saw it, for it might have made him feel uncomfortable. However, he followed me to the door and fought with me to see what it was that I was trying to hide from him. I successfully tore it off, but failed to keep my balance and fell on him. I had never been so close to him before. The previous night, he had accidentally touched my waist, but this was far more than that. I lay sprawled over him and I could feel his warm breath on my neck. What I felt inside me is inexplicable. Thank God, he helped me rise up.

I rushed out of the room, breathing very heavily. I then realised that I had forgotten his photo back in the room. 'Forget about it. What if you had stayed there? How could you have controlled your emotions?" I asked myself. I realized that staying behind the imaginary walls was tougher than I had thought. Either my emotions got hurt or his belief in me. I decided to be careful to safeguard our mutual agreement till he accepted living with me in the present. Love could be proved by loving the loved one; nothing else could do it.

The next day, everyone at home left us alone in the house. Though they made it look very casual, I sensed that it was being done intentionally. 'Nothing makes a difference here right now,'I said to myself and laughed at my fate. I walked into the kitchen and everything was already prepared for us in advance. I had no work there, so I switched on the TV. I heard Ajai calling out from the room, so I went into my room to see what he wanted. He was half sleep and was yelling to reduce the T.V.'s volume, but the really amusing part was that he said,"Maa, reduce the volume."

I turned off the T.V. and picked up a book from the shelf. After a few minutes, Ajai walked out of the room, still groggy from sleep. I laughed when he asked,"Maa, coffee?"

"Maa is not here. Can I get you some coffee?" I asked him. He then realised that he was not in his own house and covered his face with his palm.

"I am sorry. I have never stayed anywhere besides my own house," he told me.

"That's fine. Do you want coffee?" I asked him again. He nodded his head.

I recalled his preference before I started making it, so I could impress him. I handed over the coffee cup to him and went to sit next to him.

"Where is everyone?" he asked curiously.

"Everyone has left us alone," I told him. He laughed and I could read his mind. The same thoughts had come to my mind when I realised that everyone had left us. However, I decided to utilise that opportunity to build a healthy conversation with him.

"I saw your short film. It was really great," I said appreciatively.

"Really? Which one?" he asked.

"Umm...A Vision After 30 Seconds."

"That was my first short film. Everyone said that it was very unprofessionally done," he said in disbelief.

"Failure doesn't mean we are incapable. Your story was good. I look for the positive elements in everything."

"That's great! What do you do? Actually, my mom did tell me about you, but I am not able to recall it," he said, genuinely accepting his forgetfulness.

"I work for my dad business. You must remember that he runs a construction company at least," I explained.

"Are you an engineer then?" he asked, surprised.

I gave him an astonished look and asked,"So? You really don't know anything about me, do you?"

He accepted his ignorance and apologised to me for it. I then told him everything about myself and came to know even more about him. It made me realise the true reason behind my family's absence. He asked me how I had met him and how I had fallen in love with him. I took the opportunity to tell him everything from the start. Tears rolled down my cheeks when I told him about the day I had come to know about his girlfriend. For a brief moment, there was a deep silence in the room.

When I heard a knocking sound on the door, I wiped my tears and went to unlatch it. It was my mom. She walked into the house and smiled when she saw Ajai. He stood up immediately in courtesy and greeted her.

"Please take your seat, son. This is not required. Treat me as your own mother," she comforted him."Haritha, did you give him any breakfast?" she asked me in a commanding tone.

"No, mom. He woke up just a few minutes ago," I replied.

"You are useless. I should blame your dad for this. You please wait, son. I will prepare some hot *dosas*(savoury rice-pancakes) for you," she said and went into the kitchen.

Ajai laughed at me and I murmured to him,"All this is because of you. You woke up late, yet I got the scolding."

That evening, my mom mentioned how they had made arrangements for the night after the wedding. I tried to postpone it to some other day, but my mom refuted with a strong'No'. I was left with the only option to let Ajai know about this. 'I don't know how he would react to this. What will happen to the wall between us?'I asked myself. However, he laughed when I told him all about the night-after-the-wedding preparation.

"Why are you laughing?" I asked him.

"Nothing...don't worry about it. I will take the floor and you may sleep on the bed. I had expected this. We can't always sleep in different rooms, like we did yesterday," he gave the idea to sort things out.

After a few hours, my mom and some women relatives of my family guided me to my room with some fruits and milk in my hand. I felt nervous despite knowing that nothing was going to happen that night.

"God bless you, my dear," my mom said and sent me inside the room.

I walked into my room and locked the door behind me. I found Ajai sitting on the bed. I was speechless and felt too uncomfortable to remain standing. I placed the fruits and milk on a table. He took the bed spread and a pillow and placed them on the floor.

"You can sleep on the bed," he said, pointing towards the bed.

I was not able to shake off this strange feeling growing inside me. I took a seat on the bed and tried to overcome my nervousness. After sometime, I felt a little better and relaxed.

Though the season of summer was well past, I felt hot inside the room, so I switched on the AC. My own room felt new to me and I tried to sleep, but there was something that didn't let me. I heard the sound of a shivering sigh coming from below, and I realised that Ajai was feeling the chill, so I placed a blanket on him. When his shivering did not subside still, I decided to switch off the AC.

The next day, I woke up early. I awakened Ajai and asked him to sleep on the bed, so no one would suspect us not having slept together. I walked out of the room and found my mom in the kitchen.

"You look very tired. Go and get refreshed. I will get you tea," she said and smiled.

I had no clue of the reason behind her smile. Then, when I looked at myself in the bathroom mirror, I realised that I did look very tired and sweaty. 'I had switched off the AC, but it worked very well to misguide my mom,' I said to myself. I took my cloths and went into the bathroom. When I came out, I found Ajai still asleep on the bed, so I tapped on his shoulder to wake him up.

“Good morning,” he wished me.

“Good morning. Go and get ready. We need to go to the temple today. Your mom is on the way,” I informed him.

“Oh, no.She is going to kill me. I forgot to call her since I came here,” he said and rushed to the bathroom.

I closed the door and went to the living room. Meanwhile, Ajai’s mom had reached our house and my parents received her. I greeted her and took her blessings.

“How are you, Haritha? Where is he? I need to give him a slap,” she said playfully.

“Hahaha...I know it. Wait, I will call him. He is in the shower,” I replied and went into my room.

I found him standing in front of the mirror,ina towel tied around his waist. Immediately, I shifted my gaze from him, informed him about his mother’s arrival and left the room. I went back and told his mom that he would be ready shortly.

I rushed to the kitchen and drank some water to calm myself down. I had not expected to see him half naked. I felt embarrassed, feeling that he might have taken my behaviour mistakenly. I asked myself,‘Where are your manners? You are supposed to knock the door before entering.’

He came out of the room casually and greeted everyone. His mom pulled him aside and asked him whether he remembered her at all now. He pointed to me and said,“Ask you daughter-in-law. She has filled your absence.”

“No, Amma. Don’t believe him,” I said and smiled.

Chapter 19

Ajai Adithiya

I walked out of the room in the morning and asked Maa for some coffee, but Haritha reminded me that I was in her house. She offered me coffee. I soon realised that there was no one at home besides us. When I asked her about it, she said that everyone had left us alone for a while.

I felt that it was the right time to get to know more about her. I was surprised to find out that she was an engineer and managed one of her dad's companies. It added to my surprise when she mentioned having watched one of my short films and appreciated my effort too. Her positive words reminded me of my mom. She seemed very bold and an optimist to me.

"How did you come across me? When did you start developing the feeling of love for me?" I asked her.

She told me everything and I noticed tears in her eyes when she was talking about it, but she managed to hide them from me.

'Had I met you first in my life, I might have fallen for you,' I said to myself. Love never lets anyone stay happy. It rather hunts them alive. I could feel her pain for not being loved back. I felt guilty for causing such merciless pain to her.

The doorbell interrupted my thoughts. It was Haritha's mom at the door. She is a really kind and caring person. She scolded Haritha for not taking good care of me and offered to make me some hot dosa. I felt amused at the whole charade between Haritha and her mom. It reminded me of my own mother and her endless scolding sessions.

That day, Haritha's family arranged the formalities for the night after the wedding. She rushed to me and told me all about it. I suggested a plan to her that worked well for everyone, except for me. I was not able to sleep due to some weird feeling growing inside me, and that feeling accentuated even more due to the chill in the room.

She got up in the middle of the night and came next to me. I felt my heartbeat rising to its peak inside my chest. She placed a blanket over meand switched off the AC.

The next morning, I woke up early and saw that she was sweating, though asleep. I realised that she was not comfortable without an AC, but had sacrificed her comfort for me. I pretended to be asleep when she woke up.

"It is your turn now. You can sleep on the bed," she said to me and left the room.

She had all the qualities which I had expected. After my Maa, she was the only one who loved me so much. 'What is stopping you from accepting this truth?'I asked myself over and over again.

After sometime, Haritha came out of the bath and reminded me of my Maa's arrival.

I dressed up hastily for the temple visit, and went out into the living room. I found Maa there, already waiting for me.

"You've forgotten me since you've come to your father-in-law's house," she accused me.

I denied her accusation and blamed Haritha for it.

Chapter 20

Haritha

Days passed with the hope that he would understand my love towards him. We started to spend a lot of time together and explored each other's personality until the time came to rejoin our respective offices. Thing changed when he rejoined his office after the wedding.

His night shift and my general shift stood as a barrier in our married life. I hardly saw him during the weekdays. He would reach home at mid night, while I had to leave for office when he was still in deep sleep.

"Why don't you ask Ajai to change his job?" my mom asked me.

"I can't force him for it,it is his career. He never asked me to quit my job," I replied. Those words had come from my mind, but my heart still agreed with my mom.

Later that day, I found myself sitting alone at the canteen, lost in my thoughts, my cup of tea growing cold. Shoba approached me and placed her hand on my shoulder.

"Are you okay, Haritha?" she asked.

I drew myself out of the thoughts that had been haunting me.

"Yeah, I am okay," I lied to her. Real friends are able to find the truth behind our words, by the tone of our voice. She did.

"Please don't lie to me. I can sense that there is something wrong. You haven't been okay since you've come back from your wedding leave," she said and took the seat beside me.

"It's Ajai," I gave in.

"What is it with Ajai? Is there a problem between you two?" she asked in a serious tone.

"We hardly get time to spend with each other. You know,we haven'teven started our life together yet." I became emotional.

"What?"

"Yes, I agreed to be his friend till he got over his past. I thought we would get time to get to know each other better, and I believed I would be able to bring him out of his past. But now, it looks like either he or I must quit our career to make that happen." I turned to look away dejectedly.

"Oh, I thought you guys are happy. Why did you accept to be his friend?" she questioned me.

"I was left with no other option. That's what is the problem now." I looked into her eyes, with nothing else to say.

She suggested that I talk to Ajai about it and sort things out. I felt that it was a good idea.

"*I need to talk to you,*"I texted Ajai.

"*Even I do. I am coming by your office to pick you up,*" he replied.

I became both curious and overjoyed as he had never come to my office before. I awaited his arrival.

'I must use this opportunity to express everything to him. I think he is going to express his feelings for me too. Our life is finally going to start.'I remained lost in my thoughts until his bike's honk interrupt them. I blushed when he took his helmet off his head, but he looked a bit sad or rather occupied with something on his mind.

"Haritha, can we go to the beach?" he asked me.

He had never taken me anywhere since the wedding, except when forced by our parents. I had mixed emotions about it.

He parked his bike and we walked to the beach. He pulled me back by my hand when I was about to cross a road, and it spoke enough about how much he cared for me.

We sat down on the sand near the shore of Eliot's beach. A beautiful full moon was resting above the dark sea and I could hear the song of the waves. The pleasant composition of nature and cool breeze opened a window to eternity to us. I had never imagined to have a romantic datelike this with Ajai. I wished to rest against his shoulder and admire that beauty till my last breath.

"Jennifer texted me today," he said in a flat tone without shifting his gaze from the sea.

My dreams shattered like a mirror and I felt my heart growing heavy. I looked into his eyes, but they still remained looking away. I became quiet and was left with no words to speak with him further.

"But I didn't reply to her," he continued.

"Hmm..." I nodded and asked him,"Why didn't you reply to her?"

He shifted his gaze towards me and looked deep into my eyes. I could see tears welling up in his eyes, but he wiped them away.

"I've got nothing to talk to her about," he raised his voice.

I was left with no clue.'Why does he want me to know about this? Does he mean to say that I have occupied his life, so he is left with no option but to live with me?' Such questions took over my mind. I broke my chain of thoughts and asked him,"Am I stopping you form taking the next step?"

"What?" He looked at me and tried to say something, but didn't.

"If you wish, I can leave your life and you can be by yourself again."

"Please stop this nonsense. I don't want to leave you, and I... I... you are my wife. Nothing will change that," he sounded firm.

"Sorry, I thought you wanted to leave me," I confessed my insecurity to him.

"Haritha, I struggled to get over my past,but I have done it now, and I..." he said and paused.

There was a deep silence between us. My insecurity had done enough damage to him. 'Heshared the truth with me,although he could easily have hidden it, but he didn't. I would never have been able to find out about this. There is something stopping him from confessing his love to me. I need to give him some more time,'I said to myself.

A cop approached us and asked us to leave, since it was quite late. We walked out of the beach quietly. I hadn't realised how cold it wasuntil Ajai held my hand tightly in his and pulled me closer to himself.

"I will never leave you," he said to me. These words sounded more pleasant than the sea waves...

Chapter 21

Shadow From the Past

One day, I almost walked into the living room as I was feeling hungry, but stopped when I heard a conversation about my night shift between Haritha and her mom. Her mom suggested that Haritha should ask me to change my job or my shift, but she refused to do it, and defended me instead. I felt very proud of her that day. She was not ready to let me down to anyone, not even her mother.

I heard from my director after a long time that day. He had sent me some scripts to read and give him suggestions about. I opened those files in my mobile and started reading. One was a really nice script which talked about the problems faced by people in the corporate industry, particularly the people with difficult shifts. I smiled on reading that, since it reflected my own situation.

A girl's character in that script suffers a lot due to a hard shift. At one point, she is forced to pick a side between her career and a married life. She fails to express her love and loyalty to her husband. Her failure in her career and life brings her to the edge of a building from where she decides to jump and commit suicide. There ends the scene. I laughed when I finished reading the script.

'Why does he want to convey a negative storyline to the audience?'I asked myself and dialled his number.

"Hello, Sir?"

"Hi! Ajai, how are you?" he asked me.

"I am good. I have a question about the storyline."

"Yeah, tell me?"

"Why does this end so negatively?" I asked him.

"Actually, I read an article just last week about a girl committing suicide. She suffered a lot with her life and her husband hated her. That had made her take such a decision," he explained to me.

"Can't we make it end positively, sir? A girl challenging the society and its view, convincing her husband to understand her love, being able to achieve awork-life balance,perhaps?" I suggested.

"Hmm…yeah, that sounds better, but I think this negative storyline could prove her pain and love to the audience in a better way."

"Sure, we will try that," I gave in to his view since it was his story and I had to respect his creation.

We decided on a date to start our movie discussion, and disconnect the call.

I received a text message from an unknown number.

"Hey, it's Jennifer. Can we talk?"

I ignore it and felt that I should inform Haritha about it.

Later that day, I went over to Haritha's office to pick her up. She was really happy to see me, asit was my first time going to pick her up from office. I was worried about spoiling her joy, but I couldn't keep this hidden from her. She was my wife. I smiled to myself at those words.

I took her to the beach where I had had beautiful memories with Jennifer, but this time I decided to bury all those memories right there. Haritha looked very beautiful to me. The full moon's light bounced off her skin and made her seem to glow like a princess. I had never realised before how adorable she looked when she smiled. Haritha had conquered my heart with her beauty. 'What spell have you cast on me?'I admired her beautiful dark eyes.

I gathered the courage to tell Haritha about the text message, and when I finally said it, I could feel the pain inside her. I rushed to comfort her, but her response broke my heart.

I was not able to control my tears and I don't know why I felt so heavy hearted when she asked me, "Why don't you reply to her?"

'Does that mean she doesn't love me? Isn't she supposed to get angry or possessive about me?'I asked myself.

Her words had stabbed deep into my heart and I could feel it bleeding inside. She was ready to leave me so easily.

"Please stop this nonsense. I don't want to leave you, and I... I... you are my wife. Nothing will change that," I tried to explain,but my words failed to convincingly express my love for her.

I loved Haritha, but I wasn't able to confess it to her. I don't know when I had started to develop such feelings for her. I was not ready to lose her at any cost.

I looked away after explaining my state to her, but something stopped me from confessing my love to her. We were forced to leave the place by a cop. I caught her hand and held it tightly to make her feel secure. I believed that one day

I would be able to confess my love to her. She had invaded my heart and had started to rule it.

'I love you, Haritha,'I said inside my heart.

Chapter 22

Ajai Adithiya

I decided to write my first movie script, so I sat in Haritha room and started working on it. Meanwhile, Haritha walked into the room.

"I thought you typed your scripts," she said surprised.

"Hmm...writing with a pen gives me more pleasure than typing on a laptop," I explained.

"Okay, Mr. writer." She sat down beside me and started to read while I was writing.

I could smell her fragrance when she moved in too close to read what I had written. She spelled some lines out loud and said,"Your lines are really amazing." When sheleaned back to regain her position, our eyes met. I looked deep into her beautiful dark eyes. Our heads drew closer, enough that I could feel her warm breath over my lips.

Her eyes shied away and jumped around like a trapped deer. Goose bumps ran up my lower spine,all the way to my hands. I tried to control my fingers which had already taken a lead towards her. I grabbed her chin and was about to kiss her lips. We both realised that magical moment, but the very next moment, I released my grip and shifted my gaze away. 'What am I doing?'I asked myself.

I turned back to look at her, to apologise for my mistake, but it was too late. She placed a kiss on my lips. I froze with the shock of it and wasn't able to respond to her, so she broke it.

"Sorry, I broke my promise," she sounded guilty.

"Don't be sorry," I said and dropped my pen.

She tried to leave the room, but I pulled her back. I kissed her lower lip and hugged her as tight as I could. I was even able to hear her heart beat inside me. She broke away and asked me,"Is this the right way to treat your friend?"

"You are not my friend anymore," I smiled and continued to kiss her.

Tears rolled from her eyes and I wipe them. "Sorry, I've hurt you a lot," I said to her.

She hugged me close and rested her cheek over my shoulder for some time. 'This is the right time to confess my love,'I said to myself.

"Haritha, I need to tell you something," I started, but she placed a finger over my lips and said,"Not now. I don't want to break this beautiful moment."

She kissed me again and we both stayed hugging each other till a ring on my mobile interrupted us. I picked it up onlyto realise that it was just the alarm. I blinked my eyes over and over again. I then realised that I was only dreaming. I hadn't realised when I fell asleep while writing my script. Haritha came into the room and asked me to take her to a movie. I blushed and said *Yes*. She gave me a weird look and went into the bathroom. I scratched my head and laughed.

'I must confess my love to her before it gets too wild,'I said to myself.

I walked over to the living room and sat in front of the TV. Haritha walked out of her room after a while wearing a sandal coloured designer saree with a maroon border. She was trying to tie her hair up. I lost myself to the sight of her.

"What? Why are you sitting here? Go and get ready," she ordered me.

"Yes, I will." I ran into the bathroom like a school kid.

I turned on the shower and realised the heat inside me when thecool water cascaded down my frame. I dressed myself in a causal black denim jeans and a sandal coloured shirt to match with her saree. She handed over the car keys to me and said,"We will take my car out to the movie today."

"Actually, I don't know how to drive a car," I confessed sheepishly, scratched behind my head.

She laughed and said,"Okay, fine. I will drive."

"Do you know how to drive?" I asked her with surprise.

"I do, but I have never tried to drive a bike."

"Okay then, you teach me how to drive a car and I'll teach you the bike," I said, offering her my hand.

"Deal," she said and shook my hand.

That was the first time that I went to a theatre and hardly watched the movie, because I was busy staring at Haritha. I shifted my eyes away whenever she felt that my eyes were not on the screen. She even asked me about it, but I refused to accept it. I placed my hand on hers,pretending as if it happened accidentally. I knew I was her husband, but my heart felt like that of a mischievous lover.

After the movie, she took me to a street food stall and ordered *Bhel Puri* and *Mushroom Masala*. I hardly registered the taste of Mushroom Masala, even swallowed the hot mushrooms sometimes, making her laugh out at my conduct.

Chapter 23

CompromiSed WallS

I walked into my room and found Ajai sleeping over his script papers. I went to sit besidehim and started reading some of them. I soon realised that Ajai was murmuring. I stood up from the bed but found that he was asleep,yet speaking something. I became curious to hear what he was mumbling in his sleep.

"Haritha, Haritha," I heard him say, and then something else too which I was not able to comprehend easily, so I leaned in closer to him. Suddenly, he kissed me and I stood up in disbelief.

I was confused, not able to believe the moment just past. I tried to walk away from there, but he grabbed my hand very tightly. I sat beside him to release my hand from him.

"You are not my friend anymore. Sorry, I hurt you a lot," he continued to murmur.

Tears rolled down from my eyes and a drop fell on his lip. I kissed him and the wall between us was finally compromised. Those words were more than enough for me. His mobile started to ring just then and I rushed out of the room. Pretending like nothing had happened,I walked back into the room. He looked confused.

"Shall we go to a movie today?" I asked him.

He agreed and went into the living room.

I handed over the car keys to him and asked him to drive us to the movie, but he sheepishly confessed that he didn't know how to drive. I laughed and made a deal with him.

He never shifted his eyes away from me during the movie. I caught him red handed many times, but he acted innocent. His behaviour amused me. After the movie, I took him to a local chaat stall, where he amused me even more.

That night, he gave a silly excuse to turn on the A.C.

"If I switch it on, you are the one going to suffer," I said to him.

"That's fine," he replied.

He mumbled something. When I asked him about it, he mentioned that he was not comfortable sleeping on the floor. So I decided to take the floor and offered him the bed, but he refused.

"Can't we share the bed?" he asked innocently.

"What?" I replied in shock, though I knew his intentions were pure.

"No. No. That's not what I meant to say," he replied quickly, scared by the nature of my tone.

I laughed and accepted his proposal. He placed a pillow between us.

'What is he trying to do?'I asked myself and gave him a weird look.

Due to his long and tiring shift, he was not able to sleep the entire night. The next day, I found those pillows still there between us. I felt proud of his gentlemanly attitude. I kissed him again before he woke up.

I reached the office earlier than usual that day and found Shoba at her cabin.

"Wow, you are early today?" she asked me.

"I have some pending work to complete," I replied.

"Don't lie. Your face has something else to say," she figured.

I told her everything about the weekend.

"You guys need to put an end to this hide and seek, though it does sound quite romantic," she advised.

"Yeah, I am waiting for Ajai to confess his love to me," I said and nodded in assent.

I got busy with my monthly meetings and presentations to the new clients. They demanded for us to come up with even more designs. I felt that was my turn to pitch in. I promised to deliver more designs before the weekend. I skipped my lunch that day due to that presentation.

I didn't realise how time passed and before I knew it, it was already 8 PM in the evening. Some engineers and I were the only people remaining in the office. A security personnel rushed to me and handed me my mobile which I had forgotten on the table. I was surprised to see so many missed calls and text messages from Shoba and some other people. I prioritised Ajai's missed calls and texts.

"Call me once you see my text," he had texted me.

I dialled his number and he picked up on the first ring. I feared that it must be something very urgent.

"Hey! What happened to you?" He sounded restless.

"Sorry, I was in a client meeting," I apologised to him.

"Listen, I need to leave for Pune tomorrow. It's BCP testing."

I became silent.

"I know, it's very short notice. Still, it is very important so I can't avoid it," he continued.

"Okay, at what time are you leaving and for how long will you be there?" I asked, worried.

He laughed."I will be back by this weekend."

"What sounds so funny here?" I lost my temper.

That left him wordless for a minute before he apologised to me.

'I am going to miss you,'I said to myself.

"Hmm...I will miss you," he said.

"Really?" I asked in disbelief.

"Yes. I have something else to say, but you'll have to wait till I come back," he said.

"Okay," I said and we disconnected the call.

I knew what he was going to say, but I was not ready to wait for so long. However, I realised I had so much work to do that I could easily divert my attention. The next morning, I saw no pillow walls on the bed, nor him. I felt for the remains of his warmth on the bed and cried hugging his pillow.

'How could he leave me without even saying goodbye?'I asked myself and soaked the pillow with my tears.

My mobile rang and I found that it was him. I wiped my tears and cleared my throat before answering the call.

"Hello?"

"I am really sorry for not saying goodbye to you before leaving," he confessed.

"Even your friend deserves a bye, right?" I asked angrily.

"Hmm...you are not my friend anymore," he said.

"What?" I asked him. My mind reeled with the pain of these words, not able to realise what he actually meant.

"I have said more than enough. You'll need to wait till the weekend to know more," he said and disconnected the call.

I hated his suspense,although it was worth the wait. "I love you Ajai and I miss you a lot," I spoke into the disconnect call.

I became very busy with my new designing work over the next few days. I stayed in till late at office as much as I could and continued the remaining work at home. I slept for only three to four hours a day, that too on Ajai's side of the bed in my room. His scent gave me comfort in his absence.

Chapter 24

Chennai to Pune

I went to office on Monday with a deep lack of interest since it was the week's beginning and I wished to spend some more time with Haritha.

The moment I reached the office, I was informed that I would have to take a business trip to Pune the next day. I got the air tickets for the same.

I sat at my desk and looked out the window from where I could see the Chennai airport. For so long I had wished to take a flight trip, but I never got the chance before. I might have felt happy about it had I never met Haritha, but things were different now.

'I am going to miss her,'I said to myself. Though I knew it was a short trip and that I would be staying in Pune only till Friday, my heart was not prepared to leave her. I dialled Haritha several times, but she did not respond. I stared at the airport through my window. A teammate tapped on my shoulder and pointed to my mobile which was ringing. I looked at the screen and found that it was Haritha. I was worried how I would be able to explain my situation to her.

She was not happy with the news of my trip, but gave in because of its importance.

I reached home late that night and found Haritha sleeping in her room. I was left with only a few hours before the early morning flight, so I rested next to her on the bed for a while. I admired her beauty while she was in deep sleep.

I woke up after a nap and packed my luggage hurriedly. Meanwhile, Haritha's mom got up and came to the living room where I was packing.

"What happened? Where are you going?" She was astonished to see me packing up my things.

I explained everything to her.

"So, when is your flight?" she asked me.

"Hmmm...in two hours," I replied to her.

"How will you manage there? Is anyone going with you? I don't know how you are going to manage in a new town," she said, clearly worried about me.

That reminded me of my Maa and her care. I replied to all her questions and smiled.

"Okay, let me help you," she offered.

I folded all my garments and kept everything that I required for the trip inside the luggage bag. Haritha's mom helped me with it.

"I was not ready to accept you when Haritha first mentioned about her love to us," she said while arranging the things in my bag.

I gave her a shocked glance and asked, "Why? What is the problem with me?"

"Not now, prior to the wedding," she explained.

"Oh, okay.Why was that?" I asked her.

"We thought that perhaps she was too young to decide her future with someone. We got some really wealthy grooms for her, but Haritha's dad rejected them all because he was looking for good character over good money, and I agreed with him. Actually, we were not entirely sure about you either, buthe believe in his daughter and her decision more than my words."

I nodded in reply to her words and she continued, "Later, I realised how correct her decision was. You are a really good person and thank you very much for taking such good care of her." She wiped a tear of joy.

"Thank you, aunty. I will never let you down. I promise," I said and smiled.

"I know. Haritha is very stubborn. You won't believe it, she took an interview even at her dad's company before joining there. She got rejected the first time, but she didn't give up. She kept trying hard and finally cracked it. If she loves something, she will give in her maximum effort to get it."

Her words regarding Haritha really surprised me. Sitting for an interview to join her own father's company was exemplary of her simplicity and attitude. No one in the world would do such a thing. I agreed that she really was down to earth. No wonder, she got that from her family.

"I am really lucky to have Haritha in my life," I said to her mother.

She smiled and went into the kitchen to prepare a cup of coffee for me.

I looked at Haritha sleeping in her room and decided to let her sleep,since she looked very tired. I sat beside her and sipped my coffee.

"I am really sorry, Haritha. My past has ruined our present and your happiness. Thank you for choosing me as your life partner. A girl left me because of her parents and their pride, but you stood for me because of your love. Yes, I used to think that true love is only a fantasy and can never exist in real life, but you proved me wrong. I wasted our days which we spent together. Now that I am leaving you, even though it is just for a few days, I feel pain inside me. I love you, Haritha," I said,but she was still in deep sleep.

I kissed her forehead and left the house. Haritha's dad dropped me off at the airport and I waved him goodbye.

I walked into Kamaraj Domestic Terminal and placed my luggage on the luggage commuter belt near the check-in counter.

"Your name, sir?" the woman at the counter asked.

"Haritha," I replied.

"Excuse me, sir?" she asked, giving me a weird look.

I realised my mistake, but was not able to answer back as I had left my mind and heart back in Haritha's room. I simply placed my air ticket on her desk.

"Okay, sir. This is your boarding pass. Thank you for travelling with us." She handed over the pass to me and smiled.

I took a chair near Gate 5 and placed my coat beside me. I hadn't slept much since it was an early morning flight, but I had planned to reach Pune early and take rest at my office guest house, so I could avoid a last minute rush to the Pune office.

After a few minutes, I heard the call for boarding, so I joined the people waiting for the Pune flight.

"Can I have your boarding pass, sir?" an air hostess asked me.

I realised then that I had left my boarding pass and my coat back at the chair I had been sitting on. I rushed back to pick them up.

'Thank God,' I said to myself when I found my coat right where I had left it. I walked back to the gate and gave my boarding pass to her.

"Are you sure you haven't left anything else behind?" she asked sarcastically.

'Yes, a piece of my heart,' I said to myself and smiled at her.

They asked everyone to switch off their mobiles as part of the travelling protocol. I switch it off and hoped to reach Pune before Haritha woke up. Luckily, the flight landed earlier than expected. It was around 5 AM in the morning. I took a cab to Shivaji Nagar.

I found it quite difficult to guide the cab driver to my office guest house. I could understand Hindi a bit, but he was talking in Marathi. Google Maps and some of my friends helped me locate the destination and reach there. The cab and auto drivers in Pune are really worth the appreciation. They were all really kind and polite to me. Initially, I felt hesitant taking an auto there, since it is treated as a luxury in Chennai. Anything above 5 kilometres is charged a minimum of 200 rupees.

I dumped all my things on the bed and dialled Haritha.

When she said 'hello', I could tell from the tone of her voice that she had been crying. I apologised to her right away, but she was quite angry with me. I promised to give her some pleasant news on coming back home and disconnected the call. I knew that she would probably guess it, but hearing it from me would give her more joy.

My first day in Pune went very well. I met with some senior officers and co-workers with whom I needed to work during that testing.

Everything looked the same at office. Even at the guest house, it was a similar AC'droom as that of Haritha, but I missed her warm breath. I missed her fragrance and her beautiful dark eyes. I was not able to sleep that night, despite trying very hard. I took my notepad out and scribbled down some poems and her name on it. I searched through my mobile for a picture of her, but found none. I had never taken a picture of her myself.

I called Swaran to send me some of my wedding pictures that he had taken from his mobile.

I was eager to see those pictures. Never before had I known the pain of a bad internet connection as that day. Finally, the pictures arrived! I laughed upon seeing myself with that tough face. I seemed nowhere close to matching up to her beauty that day. She looked gorgeous, like the reflection of an angle. I hugged those pictures close to my heart and slept.

The next day, I got some time to visit some other places in Pune and nearby areas. I decided to avoid calling Haritha till I returned back to Chennai because I had no confidence in myself to be able to withhold the suspense. I took a cab to the Indo-Japan friendship Park which all my Pune colleagues had suggested that I should go to. The pleasant view it offered rendered me speechless. I witnessed a paradise in front of me. The greenery and the Koi fish ponds added even more beauty to it.

"I might have proposed to Haritha, had she been with me here," I said to myself.

I took as many photos as I could and soon left the place because every passing minute there tempted me to dial

Haritha. I sent some of the picture to her,captioning them with some words of love.

She called me back immediately on receiving the pictures, but I rejected her call with a message:

"Wait, till I come back. Save your words😆"

She replied to me with a sad emoji. I felt amused to see that face.

Chapter 25

Ajai Adithiya

I stared at the walls in the guest house. Now that the new town had become boring, I started to feel lonely. I counted the days remaining before I could go back.

"May I come in, sir?" The guest-house keeper asked me.

"Please," I replied.

He placed a cup on the table and left the room. I realised that it was tea. My thoughts flew me back to Chennai a few days ago.

Haritha had walked into our room with a cup of coffee. I said,"I am going to try tea today," and smiled. She gave me a weird look, which had become a routine those days. She came back with two cups of tea and sat beside me. While we sipped from our cups, I said to her, "I had never thought that tea could taste this great."

I drew out of my memories and sipped the tea at the guest house.'Haritha, I miss your tea,'I said to myself.

I enquired the room boy for a nearby place which I could visit that day and he suggested the Dagadusheth Halwai Ganapati Temple. I hadn't been to a temple since my break up with Jennifer, except for the wedding rituals. Both God and Jennifer had failed my belief in divinity. I still had those unhealed wounds inside my heart, but I had grown used to living with them now.

I took an auto to the temple. I had never seen such a colourful Ganapati in my life. I stood in line for *darshan*. The statue looked so magnificent to me that my hands joined together of their own accord.

"I compromised my life but I am happy for what I have got now. Thank you for bringing Haritha into my life," I prayed and felt positive inside.

After a nap at the guest house, I went to the office. 'Two more days to meet my love,' I consoled myself.

My Maa called me up and scolded me for not letting her know about the Pune trip. I laughed and said, "I have forgotten you since my wedding."

"I knew you would forget me, but I did not expect it to happen so early," she laughed.

"Maa, what do you want from Pune?" I asked her.

"Come back safely. That's more than enough," she said and disconnect the call.

Chapter 26

Shoba walked into my cabin with earphone plugged into her ears.

"Haritha, listen to this song I found on YouTube. I think you might love this one," she offered the earphone plugs to me.

"No, Shoba. I am not in the mood. I need to finish these things before the weekend for the clients," I said, pointing towards the drawing.

"Hmm...spare sometime for yourself too. Try this," she said,making puppy dog eyes at me.

"Okay...fine! Stop with that innocent look," I laughed and grabbed her earphones.

The song started with some nice keyboard notes, followed by the humming of a girl. I got curious to listen further. Shoba and I shared a smile.

'*Pesamal unthan mounam enthan nenjil kathal valaiye vesi siluthe.*'(A girl expresses her one sided love for a friend.)

It reminded me of Ajai and myself.

"Which movie is this?" I asked Shoba.

"It is an album actually, called *Mounam Pesum Varuthaikal.* It is trending right now."

My mobile blinked with a received message and I unlocked it. It was Ajai. He had sent me some pictures from Pune. I dialled him up immediately, but he rejected the call. I felt heart-broken.

He sent me a message,"*Wait till I come back. Save your words*😆"

'How long is he going to make me wait?'I asked myself.

I felt the pain of loneliness without him, so I kept myself occupied with the sketches and drawings for the client presentation on Friday. I decided to stay at office as long as possible because my room haunted me with his memories. I found it difficult to sleep too, since I missed his warmth next to me.

Days passed and the awaited day finally arrived. I prepared my final output for the client presentation. My dad came to attend the presentation, which added to my pressure.

"What a surprise! You are here today?" I asked my dad.

"A very important client in our field is coming to attend your presentation today," he said with his eyes full of expectations.

"Oh, really? I will do my best," I replied, trying to hide my nervousness, but he sensed it.

"Don't worry, dear. You can do this," he said, holding my hand.

Nothing can break your confidence as long as your family supports you. Luckily, I had that. I wished for Ajai to be by my side for this important day in my life. 'Everything is happening for a cause,'I consoled myself.

I entered the meeting room and found everyone already waiting for me. I excused myself for being late and started my presentation. It reminded me of my interview with the senior engineers when I had first joined.

The clients asked me far too many questions than I had anticipated and I tried to answer them as well as I could. For a few questions, my dad stepped in to help me. I couldn't guess any sign of result on their faces. Everyone got occupied with a discussion among themselves after I was done.

"We need some time to finalise the decision," they said and left the room.

I stood feeling confused and unsure about the result. An old man walked up to me and said,"You've really got talent and I am happy to do business with your company. I will send the documents tomorrow."

He placed his hand on my dad's shoulder and took him away with him. I sat in the meeting room like a student waiting for her result. After a few minutes, my dad rushed into the meeting room and congratulated me. I was still not able to understand.

"That old man was the client I was talking about. We got the contract and I am really proud of you," he said overjoyed, and continued,"I think you are now ready to take over my business, but please give me some job too. I don't want to take retirement just yet." He laughed and hugged me.

I was left with no words. Tears of joy rolled down from my eyes. "Where are you, Ajai? Come back soon," I said to myself.

The next day, I woke up early and asked my mom to prepare some special sweets and lunch for Ajay.

"You look very happy today. Your dad told me about the new contract. I feel really happy and proud of you," said mom.

"Thank you. Ajai is coming back to Chennai today. He might just be on his way home. I've got some work that needs to be done. Please tell him that I will be back soon," I said in a rush.

"Why don't you call him andtell him that yourself?" she asked me.

"Hahaha, Maa, you won't understand," I blushed and rushed out of the house to my car.

I was filled with excitement. I played the song which Shoba had made me listen to. I could hear my own heart beats, my heart was thumping so loudly. I imagined how Ajai would propose to me when he got back and how magical that moment would be between us.

Everything looked fogged and slow to me. Suddenly, I heard the screeching sound of a truck's breaks in front of me and realised that something was terribly wrong. I floored the break pedal of my own car, but it was too late. The last thing I heard was a loud crash and the sound of people screaming.

I blinked my eyes over and over again to regain my vision. I felt a stabbing pain in my head and sticky blood running over my cheek. I wiped it off but the bleeding didn't stop. I didn't realize when I lost consciousness, but the last thing I recalled before closing my eyes was Ajai's face.

Chapter 27

Frozen Minutes

A weird feeling housed inside my chest, preventing me from falling asleep. My flight back to Chennai was still a few hours away. I rehearsed proposing my love toHaritha again and again.

"*Saab, aap apne girlfriend ko propose karnevaale hein kya?*" the room service boy asked me upon seeing my weird act.

I simply replied with a smile.

I packed everything up in my bag. My gaze suddenly fell upon a plastic bag kept near the TV stand. I opened it and found the gifts which I had bought for Haritha from Pune.'How could I forget these things?'I chided myself and took those gifts out of the plastic bag. It was a terracotta elephant car hanging, and a handmade band with her name on it. Each bead of the band contained a letter of her name. I let my fingers slide over the beads, feeling the letters of her name under my fingertips.

"I love you, Haritha," I said and placed the band close to my heart. I kept all those gifts back inside the plastic bag safely and kept the parcel with the hand luggage.

"Sir, your cab has come," the room boy called out.

I looked at the watch and said 'Just a few more hours'to myself. I handed over a hundred rupees note to him as tip and thanked him. He loaded my bags inside the cab's trunk and waved goodbye.

'Pune, thank you. I will meet you soon when I come back with my Haritha,'I said to myself when I reached the airport.

I saw the same air hostess at the gate. She smiled when I approached her.

"Is there anything you've left behind today?" she teased me.

"No, I am heading to my love whom I had left behind in Chennai," I replied to her with a big smile on my face.

"Wow, that's really nice. Enjoy the trip back home,*machan,*" she smiled.

I was pleasantly surprised when she used the word'*machan*'.I thanked her and took my seat.

I was excited to see Haritha and felt really nervous about proposing to her. After the take off, the air hostess came to me with the food trolley.

"What would you like to have,sir?" she asked me.

"Tea, please," I replied.

"Why are you laughing? Is there something wrong with my makeup?" she asked me.

"No, I am going to meet my newly married wife after a week and I am overjoyed about that," I confessed to her. Sometimes when we are excited about something, we become very friendly with everyone.

"Hahaha...she must be really lucky!" She gave me a jealous look.

"Actually, it is me who is lucky to have her in my life," I said.

"Hmm...here is your tea. Enjoy, *machan.*" She handed me the cup and moved forward.

After a few minutes, I could see the beautiful view of Marina beach out of my window. The flight took a few rounds around it. When I asked a co-passenger about it, he told me,"It will take a few rounds over the city before it gets the signal to land."

'This is really testing my patience,'I said to myself and started to tap my feet out of impatience. I did that whenever I got too tensed. Finally, the flight landed at the Chennai airport. I hurried to the gate with my hand luggage.

"Wait, sir. Don't rush. I know you are excited to meet your wife, but please slow down. Don't hurt yourself,"the air hostess warned me.

However, I was not ready to listen to those words. I smiled and rushed to the luggage collection area regardless. I grabbed my luggage without wasting so much as a minute, and hopped onto a cab for home. I called up on Haritha's number to inform her that I was on my way home, but she didn't respond. I guided the driver towards home, but the cab got stuck in traffic which refused to move even an inch. 'Not again,'I said to myself.

I lost my patience at last and got down to check what was causing the traffic. A few meters away on the opposite road, I saw an ambulance and a crowd gathered around. I always felt sick upon seeing such kind of accidents, since they reminded me of my dad. I walked back to the cab.

"What happened,sir?" the driver asked me.

"An accident has happened over there. Can we take the parallel ECR?" I suggested.

He nodded in agreement and looked for a street to reach the ECR. Meanwhile, I dialled Haritha again. The call got picked up, but I heard a male voice on the other end of the line. I looked at my phone's screen to confirm that I had indeed dialled the right number, but it was her number.

"May I know who this is? I am Ajai and this is my wife's number," I spoke into the phone.

"Sir, this is the sub inspector speaking. Please head to Adyar Hospital right away. They took her to the hospital just a few minutes ago," he said.

I lost the grip on my mobile and dropped it. I looked back at the accident spot. A cop was standing away from the crowd and talking over the mobile. I ran towards him.

"What happen to her? Please tell me that she is okay!" I begged him.

"Are you Ajai? Sir, here is your wife's mobile. Sorry, I don't know what happened exactly. A few people got injured..." Before he could finish talking, I ran over to the spot of the accident.

I recognised her car, although it had got damaged terribly. All the windows were broken and there was blood all over the front seat. I collapsed to the ground with tears in my eyes. The cop rushed over to me and raised me up.

"Sir, please don't worry. Everything will be okay," he tried to console me.

"Where is she now? Where is my Haritha?" I cried.

"Adyar Hospital," he said.

Meanwhile, my cab driver arrived at the scene.

"Sir, I know where the hospital is. I will take you there." He held me by my shoulders and lead me back to the cab. He drove as fast as he could to the hospital. Meanwhile, I sat in the cab silently, feeling like a dead person. I tried to recall her face, but all I could remember were her beautiful dark eyes and the fragrance which had won my heart overthat night before the wedding on the terrace.

"Sir, don't worry. Everything will be okay," the cab driver said as we neared the hospital. He pointed towards the hospital entrance when we reached. I drew myself out of my thoughts and her memories which were so fresh as if it had all happened only a few minutes ago. The fear of losing her sent chills down my spine.

I hurried into the hospital.

"A girl met with an accident today and…and…she got admitted here," I forced the words out of me.

"First floor ICU, sir," the receptionist said, pointing towards the stairs.

I ran to the first floor like a mad man. A janitor was sweeping blood stains off the floor there. I rested against the wall and dropped down to the floor. "Oh, my God...what happen to her?" I covered my face with my hands and cried.

A nurse walked out of the ICU ward and I rushed to her.

"What happened to Haritha? Is she okay?" I asked her.

"I don't know her name, but she is a bit critical. Please check with the doctor," she said and left.

That word 'critical' almost made my heart stop. 'Why is it always me? Why does everyone leave me to be lonely?'I asked myself. 'Because of you...you made this happen to her…it is your bad luck which takes your loved ones away from you,'I cursed myself and cried.

"Haritha! Haritha! Please don't leave me," I pounded the floor and cried.

"You are Ajai, right?" a doctor asked me.

I raised my eyes and nodded at him.

"What happen to you? Why are you crying?" he asked with a weird expression.

"My wife met with an accident and she got admitted in the ICU," I replied with a broken voice.

"Haritha?" he asked me again.

"Yes," I nodded and wiped my tears.

"Are you mad? She is not in the ICU. She got injured, but she is okay now," he scolded me.

"Are you sure? I saw blood stains on her car," I asked doubtfully.

"Hmm…yeah, she got injured and had some bleeding, but she is good now," he explained.

I wiped my face with my palm and asked,"Where is she now?"

"Go to the ground floor, room number104," he said and directed me to her ward.

I followed him quietly. Her face was the only thing I wished to see at that moment. He knocked at a door and opened it after a voice said,"Come in". I knew that voice,it belonged to my Haritha.

I rushed up to her, took her hands in mine and cried out loud.

"Look at your husband. He thought you were critical and was crying in front of the ICU alone," he said and left the room.

"I saw your car and got so worried," I kissed her palm and cried.

"Look at me, Ajai. I am okay. Please don't cry," she tried to console me, but I was not able to control my emotions which flooded out as tears over my cheeks.

"I love you, Haritha. I am really sorry for hurting you," I looked into her eyes and said.

"Finally! You really made me wait for too long." She released her hand from my grip and slapped me playfully.

We both laughed.

"So? Do you love me?" I asked her.

"Yes of course, stupid," she blushed.

I cupped her face in my hands and kissed all over it.

"You remind me of my cousin's puppy which always licks my face wet," she laughed and pushed me away.

"Am I a puppy? Now I will show you what a puppy does," I said and jumped over her.

Chapter 28

A Few DayS After

"Ajai, hurry up. It's getting late," I shouted at Ajai as he struggled with the suitcases, trying to balance all of them at once.

"Are you sure we need to carry these many bags?" he asked.

"Yes, I have already decided on separate dresses for each and every location in Pune," I explained.

"I don't know how to carry these many bags." He gave me an exhausted look.

I pointed towards the trolley wheels under the bag and helped load all the luggage intothe car. Dad then dropped us at the airport.

"Are you serious that we are going to Pune for our Honeymoon?" he asked me with an innocent look on his face.

"Why? Don't you remember what you did to me at the hospital? I can't keep myself safe from you. We better finish it in Pune," I argued with him.

"Hmm...why can't we wait and plan it for somewhere else?" he acted like a kid again.

I took a deep breath and looked him in the eye. "Do you remember this mark which you gave me last night?" I asked him.

"Okay fine," he nodded. I loved that innocent look on his face.

"Look who is here again!" An air hostess exclaimed on seeing Ajai, and he blushed in return.

I gave her a smile and walked towards our seats.

"What is it between you and her?" I asked Ajai in a threatening tone.

"Nothing! Haritha, trust me, I met her the last time on my flight to Pune and mentioned to her about you," he confessed. Though I never doubted him, I found it amusing to play with him like that. I love him a lot and will always love him. He is always mine.

We landed in Pune and after checking-in to our hotel, I took him to the Indo-Japan friendship park. There, I tortured him to take photos of me at each and every corner of the park.

"Please, Haritha, I am tired," he begged.

His innocence amused me, but I was really happy for his love.

I requested the hotel to prepare our room like a honeymoon suit. Back at the hotel, I asked him to close his eyes and then took him into the room. I latched the door shut and then asked him to open his eyes. He got surprised."Did you do this, Haritha? I took you for an innocent deer, but you turned out to be a tigress," he said and we both laughed.

We jumped onto the bed and he took me in his arms and hugged me tight.

He kissed me and said,"Our first kiss."

"Actually, it's our second kiss," I laughed.

"How?" he asked, puzzled.

"Don't you remember? That day when you were writing your script, I kissed you," I confessed my mischief to him.

"Oh, I thought it was only a dream."

"I left a bit of a mark on your lip too. Didn't you realise it?" I asked him.

"Is it?" He searched for the mark on his lip.

"Please, stop this examination," I pushed his hand away from his lip.

"It is my turn now to place a mark," he said and kissed me. I respond to him likewise.

His warm breath caressed my neck and I felt a jolt of current run down my spine. He came onto me and kissed all over my face. I looked deep into his eyes. He kissed me over my eyelids and said, "These beautiful dark eyes have dragged me to you."

I hugged him tightly and felt like I was on seventh heaven.

Finally, we made love.

True love never ends in bed. It lives on till we breathe our last breath together.

Chapter 29

A Few YearS After

Ajai and Haritha were blessed with a baby girl. She has her mom's beautiful dark eyes and her dad's smile. They love each other very much and have a lot of fights, but they never leave each other alone. Those fights always end in deep kisses and kisses always lead them to bed. They make love a lot and love each other happilyforever.

Haritha was honoured with the Women Entrepreneur Award by OMR Builders Association and her company went on to get bigger clients. She is now busy with her career and her little princess. Her little princess said the same words which Haritha had told her dad when she was a kid.

Haritha's dad took his retirement and loves to play happily with his granddaughter. Haritha's mom is still busy taking care of her family, and is happy with the newly added member.

Shoba got married to Haritha's classmate and they went to Pune for their honeymoon, as suggested by Haritha. She also gave Shoba some ideas regarding torturing her new husband,just as she had tortured Ajai with clicking her pictures.

Ajai started his film career with his own script. He got a call sheet form 'Vijaysethupati'and he is now acting as a police cop who handles a mysterious corporate suicide case in Ajai's movie.

Ajai's Maa started to look for an alliance for her younger son. She compared each and every prospective bride with Haritha. She would say,"You know how perfect my elder daughter-in-law is? I am looking for someone just like her for my younger son."

Parents!

Author's Note

Life is full of surprises. Don't lose hope due to some disappointments, and never settle down. Scars from the past help you understand the real people in your life, so feel proud of carrying them.

It took me years to find out who I am and what I am. I don't know still if this is what I truly am? I run constantly behind those questions and try to seek answers for them.

Remember one thing in your life,'You are the hero of your own story, not someone else's.'So never work for someone else's dream. Work for your own dream. Sometimes, you need to prove yourself to you first, than to someone else.

Thank you very much for reading this story. These were just a bunch of words to begin with, but it got its value because of you. I will be happy to see your reviews, positive or negative. Feel free to let me know.

Facebook: www.facebook.com/AuthorAjayVinodh/

Instagram: @ajay_vinodh

E-mail: ajayvino@gmail.com

Dhanushri Foundation

A Facebook Group which is created in remembrance of a 3 years old little girl who lost her life due to a lack of financial support for her medical treatment. As a member of that Facebook Group, I have decided to share 10% of the profit from this book with them. They support economically backward children's medical treatment without any major sponsors.

Feel proud for being a part of humanity.

Thank you...